Now Is Not Too Late

Now Is Not Too Late
by Isabelle Holland

Lothrop, Lee & Shepard Books
New York

2   3   4   5   6   7   8   9   10

Library of Congress Cataloging in Publication Data

Holland, Isabelle.
    Now is not too late.

    SUMMARY: While spending the summer with her grandmother on a Maine island, eleven-year-old Cathy learns a great many things about herself and her relationship with other people.
    [1. Interpersonal relations—Fiction. 2. Grandmothers—Fiction. 3. Mothers and Daughters—Fiction] I. Title.
PZ7.H70830No   [Fic]   79-22610
ISBN 0-688-41937-2   ISBN 0-688-51937-7 lib. bdg.

one

"The Wicked Witch lives that way," Marianne said, pointing to the path that forked up to the hill.

"What wicked witch?"

"Like I said, the one that lives up the hill."

"I never heard of any wicked witch on the island."

Marianne looked smug. "I guess, since you only got here two days ago, you don't know about her. She came last week." For once, Marianne knew something I didn't. It was usually the other way around.

Marianne's pleased expression irritated me. But I decided to play it very cool. "Okay," I said. "Let's go see her."

Marianne didn't say anything, but she looked unhappy, as though she wished she hadn't brought the subject up. Finally she said, "Mother says I shouldn't."

"Don't tell her."

She looked even more unhappy. Marianne is my summer best friend and I like her most of the time, but she is inclined to be obedient.

"Do you tell her everything?" I asked.

"Of course not."

"Well—"

"It's all right for you," Marianne said. "All you have is a stepmother. That's different. Telling a stepmother a . . . a fib isn't the same as telling your real mother one."

I was about to deny it when I thought maybe she was

right. And, actually, I don't lie. I just manage not always to tell everything I know.

"I didn't say *lie* to her," I said. "I just said you don't have to tell her that we went to see the Wicked Witch. But if it's going to give you a problem, then I guess I'll just go some other time by myself."

"Anyway," Marianne went on, "you don't even have your stepmother here this summer. You're just staying with your grandmother. And that's not the same at all."

"You don't know my grandmother," I said.

"Yes, I do. I've been to her house lots of times, this summer and last summer and the summer before that and—"

"I didn't mean that, I meant . . ."

"Well," Marianne said as I hesitated, "what did you mean?"

Marianne and I are the same age. We're both eleven. But sometimes I feel a lot older. Laura, my stepmother, says it's because I'm a smart aleck from New York. Since she lives in New York, too (naturally, since we all live together), and was smiling when she said it, I couldn't really take offense. "I mean," I said now to Marianne, "that my grandmother is not your everyday, TV-serial-sweet-cookie-making grandmother."

"She makes lovely cookies," Marianne said. "You remember that party—"

I sighed. "Never mind. Let's go on home. I can go see the Wicked Witch when you're not along so your conscience won't bother you."

Marianne didn't say anything as we trudged along the path and down on the pebbly shore. Then, finally, when we got to Marianne's house, she said offhandedly, "If you do go, you'll let me know what she's like, won't you?"

6

"I don't think that would be in the spirit of being honest," I said, feeling mean. "After all, I'm taking all the risks."

"What risks?"

"There've got to be risks. Why else wouldn't your mother let you go there?"

"Well, you know how Mother is. She won't let me do anything unless she's sure it's one-hundred percent all right."

"Why doesn't she think the Wicked Witch is all right? And anyway, why does everybody call her the Wicked Witch?"

Marianne shrugged. "It started with some of the older kids, the day she got here. There's no road to the cottage, just a path. So she pushed her things up from the road in the big flat cart the market delivers things in. Anyway, there she was on the main road with the cart piled full of funny-looking stuff, a cat in one of those see-through carriers on top, dogs with their leashes tied to the cart, and a funny pointy hat on her head, just like a witch's. Eric Wilson and my brother Pete and a couple of the others were coming down the path from the beach on the other side. I don't know exactly what happened, but you know what a show off Eric can be, especially when he thinks he's being funny. Pete says he blocked the path and, when she asked him to move, he tried to snatch the cat or one of the dogs or something. Well, she whacked him with a king-sized umbrella. He told her she looked like a witch, and she said that was because she was one, and if he gave her any more flak, she'd put the evil eye on him."

"Pooh, she was only kidding."

"Yeah, I know. But my mother knows something else

about her and won't let me even think of going up there."

"What does your mother know?"

"I dunno. But she says it's something pretty awful. Nothing to do with being a witch, or even with all those animals she has."

I didn't say anything for a minute. It's not the kind of thing I admit to everybody, but I'm not too crazy about animals. Daddy and I had never had any until he married Laura and I acquired a stepbrother, Laura's son, Andy. Along with Andy we got Ruggles, a golden retriever.

"Lots of people have animals," I said now. "There's nothing strange about that. We have a dog at home."

"Yes, but you only have one. We have a dog, too, and two cats. But the Wicked Witch has *dozens*. I have to go in for lunch now."

"Okay. I'll see you later."

I continued along the rocky beach that curved around the bay. The air was sharp and crisp, the sun bright. The water, which was lapping a few inches from my feet, was deep blue and cold. Behind the pebbles and rocks were spruce and fir trees, some of them coming almost down to the water. Above the trees was a fairly high hill, one of several on the island. My grandmother's house is on the opposite side of the bay from the Proudys', Marianne's family. From Granny's house, which is on a sort of point, you can see the ocean on one side, on the other, the coastline of Maine and, far up, the shoreline of Nova Scotia.

Marianne and her family come to the island every summer and spend the whole season in their house there. I usually spend the summer here with my family, too. But we stay with Granny, Daddy's mother, at her summer house. This summer, though, I was staying alone with

Granny for the first few weeks. I wasn't supposed to come here at all until much later, because I was invited to go camping out West with the family of my all-year-round best friend, Janet. And, while I was doing that, Daddy and Laura were going to go to Europe and visit a lot of music festivals. Both he and Laura teach at a university in New York. Daddy teaches philosophy and Laura teaches English. They both love music and he explained to me that he and Laura hadn't had a long vacation, just to themselves, since they got married, three years before.

"We would have waited another year or two," Laura had said. "But then this invitation to you from Janet and her family came along, so we thought we'd go this year."

"What about Andy?"

"He's going to that camp that all his friends like, the one he's been nagging us about for a couple of years."

I felt a little pang of jealousy. But, after all, I was going camping, too.

"Ruggles?" I asked.

"He'll be fine. Andy almost refused to go to the camp when he learned he couldn't take Ruggles. But Ruggles will have his own vacation back at the farm where we bought him. He'll have huge grounds to run around in and a family that loves him almost as much as we do. And, after all, it's only for a month. Then we'll pick up everybody, including Ruggles, and go to your grandmother's for the rest of the summer." Laura looked at me for a minute. "I'm surprised you're so concerned about Ruggles. I had the feeling you were not that interested in him."

I shrugged. "I'm just not that into animals. The way Andy goes on about him—but then, he's a boy."

"Well," Laura said, "I don't think a fondness for animals comes with any one sex. Maybe if you had a puppy or kitten of your own—"

"I don't need one," I said. And then went on, because I really found the whole subject very boring, "I think it's terrific that you and Daddy are having a long vacation. I hope you have a great time."

She grinned. "We'll try."

But a couple of weeks before we were all due to leave, Janet woke up in the middle of the night with a bad pain, and the next thing anyone knew, she was in the hospital having her appendix out. So the whole trip had to be put off until the following year. Laura and Daddy offered to cancel their trip, even though arrangements had been made and some things already paid for. But I said they didn't have to do that. I'd just go to Granny's early. Laura, who has what Daddy calls a dry sense of humor, said that would be a Noble Sacrifice. Her hazel eyes were scrunched up at the corners, so I knew she was making a joke.

"Considering that Cathy has to be dragged away from the island each summer, kicking and screaming, I don't see what's so noble or sacrificial about it," Daddy said.

I didn't think he really had to say that, even though it was true, so I pretended to ignore it. We were sitting in the study at home, where there are sofas and bookshelves to the ceiling and a piano and a television set. Daddy and I were sitting on one of the sofas. He leaned over and pulled my hair, which I have in two short ponytails, one over each ear. "All right, Blondie," he said. "Don't pretend you haven't heard." When he isn't think-

10

ing about philosophy, or the book he's writing, or even just thinking about thinking, which is something Laura says philosophers do, he's fun. The trouble is, most of the time he's thinking.

He calls me Blondie because I'm the only blonde in the house. Laura's hair is dark brown, Daddy's is black and Andy's and Ruggles' are both red, though not the same shade. Andy's is red red. Ruggles' is sort of copper.

Andy is twelve and a half, a year older than me. Since Laura and Daddy got married and we all lived together, he's been my favorite person in the world. If somebody asked me why, I'm not sure I could say. He's not good-looking. He doesn't look like a movie or TV star, and he's shorter than I am. I'm kind of tall for my age and very skinny, and Andy's short and square. But when he says he's going to do something, he does it. He doesn't get mad over little things and, most of all, he doesn't treat me different when he's with a bunch of boys from when we're alone, the way the brothers of some of my friends do. I once asked him who his favorite person in the world was, and he said, "Ruggles." Which has always made me a little jealous.

"What about Laura?" I asked.

"I like her a lot, too," Andy said. And that's all he'd say.

I wish, I thought now, as I made my way up the pebbly path to Granny's house, that he were here now instead of at camp.

Granny's house is white frame, with a wing to one side and a big screened-in porch running around it. I often sleep out on the porch downstairs, especially when it gets warmer. Granny's father built the wing a long time ago, and *his* father built the house. I love our apartment in New York, but I like this house even better. Granny comes up from New York early in the year and stays until November. She loves the house, too.

I ran up the porch steps and into the big square hall. "Hi," I yelled.

There was no answer, so I looked first in the living room, then in the big study behind it, and finally in the dining room, where I found Granny bringing a plate of popovers out of the kitchen.

"Scrumptious!" I said. "Did you make those?"

"I did. Sit down."

I slid into my seat and put my napkin on my lap. "I yelled hi when I came in. Didn't you hear me?"

"I did. But I wasn't about to yell back. I've told you before, I don't believe in yelling from room to room and I wish you didn't either. Have a popover. Alice is going to bring in the stew in a minute."

"You're very old-fashioned," I said, buttering the popover. Then I looked at her and away again quickly to see if she was mad.

"I am delighted to say that I am. I'm sorry you don't approve."

She looked up then and we smiled at each other. Granny has dark brown eyes, a thin face, an arched nose and short, wavy, gray-black hair. I'm a little scared of her. I said that once to Daddy and Laura. And Daddy said, "Who isn't?"

"But she's your mother," I said.

"I know that very well." He glanced at me. "Don't misunderstand me, Cathy. I love her very much and always have. But I've always been a little afraid of her. After all . . . ." And then he stopped.

12

"After all, what?" I said, after a minute.

"Nothing," he said.

There was a funny, tight silence. Then Laura said, "Your grandmother is a remarkable woman, Cathy. In her lifetime, she's met most of the dragons and survived without losing her sanity or compassion."

"What dragons?" I asked.

"Fear, death, pain and disillusionment," Daddy said.

"What—" I started.

But at that moment something—I don't know what— interrupted: Andy and Ruggles came into the living room or the phone rang or Laura got up and went into the kitchen or guests arrived. I don't remember exactly.

That conversation had taken place about a year before, when we were talking about Granny and coming up to the island for the summer. I remembered it now as I looked at her over my popover. This is the first time, I thought, Granny and I have been alone together. And so I've never really known her the way you know some- body when just the two of you are together.

"Why are you looking at me in that speculative way, Catherine?" Granny said.

"I was thinking about something Laura said about you."

"Pleasant, I hope."

"She said you had fought all the dragons and come through, and Daddy said that the dragons were death and fear and pain and . . . and something else. I can't quite remember."

"That's quite an endorsement."

"What did they mean?" I asked, feeling brave.

"I suppose they meant that I had lost both your grandfather and one of my children—a daughter—and

13

that comprised death and fear and pain."

"How did they die?"

"They drowned when they were out in a sailboat."

"Out in the sea there?" I waved an arm towards the ocean.

"Right out there," Granny said. "The tides can be treacherous."

I thought about that. "It must have been pretty horrible," I said.

"It was."

"I wish I could remember what the other thing was, the fourth dragon."

"It will probably come to you sometime. Did you and Marianne have a good time this morning?"

"Yes." Suddenly I remembered the Wicked Witch. "Granny, who is the Wicked Witch?"

Granny stared at me. "Are you talking about the Wicked Witch of the West? In a book or story?"

"No. Marianne said somebody lives up the path that leads through the woods to the hill. She said everybody here calls her the Wicked Witch because she lives alone and has a lot of animals and acts strange. And also because of what happened with Eric Wilson." And I told her what Marianne had told me.

"Oh," Granny said.

There was a silence. Then, "I suppose they're talking about Elizabeth . . . Mrs. O'Byrnne. She's rented old Mrs. Hillman's cottage for the month. She's living there alone, which nobody has done for some time—certainly not a woman—since it's so remote, and she does have a tendency to collect stray dogs and cats and try and find them homes. I suppose I shouldn't be surprised that

14

this, combined with Eric's bizarre sense of humor, automatically makes her into a witch."

"Well, Marianne's mother says she shouldn't go there."

"She's quite right. If Elizabeth deliberately took a remote cottage to be alone, then she wouldn't welcome unsolicited visitors."

"What's 'unsolicited'?"

"Uninvited."

I suddenly realized that Granny had referred to the Wicked Witch as "Elizabeth." "Do you know her?"

There was a tiny pause. "I've known her for thirteen or fourteen years, although I haven't seen her for the past five."

"What's she like?"

"Really, Cathy, I don't know how to answer that. I don't know what she's like. She paints."

"But why does Marianne's mother think she shouldn't go up there? What does she know about her?"

"Perhaps you'd better ask her," Granny said coolly.

She knew perfectly well I wouldn't. I didn't like Mrs. Proudy, and if I did ask her, she'd probably say it was something little girls shouldn't discuss. Mrs. Proudy says that about most of the interesting subjects in the world. Instead, I asked Granny, "Why are you mad?"

"Because I don't like silly questions that I can't answer. Do you want another popover?"

"Yes."

"Yes what?"

"Yes, please."

Granny handed over the basket and pulled open the napkin. I took another popover and tried to think of some way to ask some more questions about the Wicked Witch that wouldn't make Granny cross. Finally I said, "What kind of things does she paint?"

"I have no idea. Are you and Marianne going to play this afternoon?"

"I guess so."

"If you want to go over to the mainland and back on the ferry, I have a couple of errands you can do for me over there. The library is holding some books for me and you can pick up some things at the dry goods store. I'll telephone an order and give you the money. I'll also treat you and Marianne to a soda."

"Thanks, Granny," I said.

Going on the ferry was always fun, and Granny never minded my going by myself or with Marianne because it was a short ride and she trusted Captain Parker, who runs the ferry. But it was a little odd that she offered to buy sodas for Marianne and me. Granny doesn't think much of sugar and junk food. I looked at her and thought about commenting on it. And then decided not to. Granny's pretty sharp. If I reminded her what she thought about sweets, she might take it back. Still, it was funny.

Alice, Granny's all-around helper, who has lived with Granny for years, brought in the dessert, which was apples and cheese.

"Hello, Alice," I said.

"Hello, Cathy."

Alice is short and rather square and has round blue eyes. She stared at me through her rimless glasses. "I've put some clean blouses and shirts on your bed. If you'll put one of them on, I'll take the one you're wearing from you and put it in the washing machine this afternoon. It's a disgrace."

I looked down my front. Marianne and I had lain on some rocks this morning and there were green and brown stains all down my sweat shirt. Still, I thought it would keep until I had to put on a clean shirt and sweater for dinner. "Can I give it to you this evening?"

"I'll not have you going out this afternoon letting everyone think I let you wear dirty clothes. Give it to me straight after lunch and I'll wash it."

"Do I have to?" I asked Granny.

"Certainly you do," Granny said.

As I tramped upstairs after lunch to change my sweat shirt I thought I might have saved my breath. Granny always supports Alice. Still, I didn't want to take my shirt off. It's my favorite, because it has a large red apple on the front with the words I LOVE NEW YORK in blue beneath. And I particularly wanted to wear it this afternoon, stains and all, because I always wear it when I have a special project on foot. If Granny was willing to bribe me with an ice cream soda, it meant she was trying to distract my attention from the Wicked Witch. And that made the witch twice as interesting, because Granny is not like Mrs. Proudy and never makes a point of forbidding me to do things on principle. As I brushed the front of my sweat shirt, I figured there was no reason I shouldn't carry out my project before I picked up Marianne to go on the ferry. I could have the soda *and* visit the Wicked Witch.

two

It was a steep climb, steeper than I remembered. I had been on the hill before, of course, but not this part of it. The path came up through the trees and wound around the side of the hill with a terrific view of the ocean just beneath. The sun, which had been bright before lunch, had gone under a cloud. The sky was gray and the water beneath the hill was a cold blue-gray. The wind had a bite in it, and I wished that I had done what Granny had suggested: brought my sweater. But I had thought I wouldn't need it. I'd been a little afraid that she would send me back upstairs to change my sweat shirt, besides making me collect my sweater, when she saw me coming downstairs. She was sitting in the living room then, writing a letter, but she didn't raise her head, and I nipped out the front door before she really took in the fact that I hadn't obeyed her. Once, Marianne asked me why I like disobeying Granny since I said I was so fond of her. And the truth was, I didn't know. I just told Marianne that a person had to keep her end up and stick up for her rights. Which sounded all right, but was the first thing I could think of.

Now, pushing my sneakers along the dirt path, I wished that I had at least taken the sweater, but it wasn't any use thinking about it now. Then I rounded the curve of the hill and went into a little hollow, which was partly shielded from the wind and was much quieter. But it wasn't quiet for long. A large black dog was heading

18

straight towards me, barking ferociously. I stood absolutely still, my heart beating. I was so scared I couldn't have moved if I'd had to.

"He won't hurt you," a voice said. "He's all noise."

"Why don't you tie him up?" I said, watching the dog run back. I knew that I sounded sharper than I'd meant to. But I don't like people to see that I'm scared and I was afraid she had.

"Because he's doing his job. He's a watchdog, and people who come around with no good on their minds don't know that he's really a cream puff."

I saw her then as she came out from the shelter of her doorway and put her hand on the big black dog's head.

I don't really know what I'd expected—maybe an old hag-like woman with nose and chin meeting and a wart with a hair coming out, just the way a lot of the books show witches. And, of course, wearing a witch's hat. So I wasn't prepared for a tall woman in jeans and a shirt and light hair in a sort of twist at the back. She was in the shadows of the house and I couldn't see her face too clearly.

Somehow I had thought of the cottage as a kind of shack. But it was really a small New England saltbox. The dog was quiet, its head under the witch's hand. I walked forward slowly, in case something made it mad again. But it stayed where it was. Then the woman came forward a step out of the shadows, so that the light fell on her face, and I was so surprised I stopped where I was. She was really beautiful. She wasn't young, but she wasn't old like Granny. Maybe forty, I thought. Her eyes were much bluer than the sea and her hair was a kind of light mouse color. I knew she was at least forty, because she had a lot of lines in her face. And even though she was smiling, there was something about her that made me think she might be sad underneath.

We stared at each other for what seemed a long time.

"You're Cathy Barrett," she said.

"Yes." I wondered how she knew.

She said quickly, "I know your grandmother. She described you."

"Oh. Granny said you're Mrs. O'Byrnne. She said she's known you for years and years."

"That's right. I'm Elizabeth O'Byrnne." She looked at me for a minute. "What else did your grandmother tell you?"

"Oh, nothing much. That you picked up a lot of animals, that you've rented the Hillman cottage for the summer and live here alone and paint."

"Does your grandmother know you're here?"

"Not exactly."

"What do you mean by 'not exactly'?"

"She wanted me to go over to the mainland to do some errands for her. She didn't *forbid* me to come."

"I see."

I looked up at her and saw that there was a sort of smile in one corner of her mouth.

"But she knew you were coming?"

"I guess so . . ."

She was looking at me in a funny way, so I said, "What kind of things do you paint?"

"Come in and see."

The front door opened straight into a big room that took up almost all the house.

"This is where I paint," she said.

There wasn't much furniture in the room, but there

were pieces of paper stuck on the walls with pins and square frames stacked on the floor. And in one corner by itself was the tall witch's hat. It was black, with funny markings on it and a narrow brim. I went over and started looking at the paintings.

Some were of the sea, a lot were of animals, and almost as many were of children. On one piece of white wall were six small paintings of a dark-haired little boy and a small black and white dog. Three of the paintings also contained a witch wearing the witch's hat.

"Why do you paint witches?" I said. I didn't really care, but I wanted to say something. The woman just standing there, watching me look at the paintings, was making me nervous.

"Those are . . . those are illustrations for a children's book," she said. I turned and looked at her, because her voice sounded funny. She was blowing her nose. "I'm sorry," she said, sounding normal. "I'm just getting over a cold."

"Oh." I turned back to the pictures. "Is that why you have the witch's hat over there?"

"Yes. I knew I would have to paint a traditional-looking witch, so I got the hat from a costume store. I like to paint from actual models as much as possible."

"Is it true you whacked Eric Wilson with an umbrella?"

The smile reappeared. "Is he the teenager with muscles and blonde hair?"

"Yes."

"Then I'm afraid it is true. First he blocked the path when I was trying to push the cart up the hill and wouldn't move when I asked him. Then he grabbed Susan's carrier and she let out a squawk. I felt she'd suffered enough traveling up here, so I told him to put it down. He just stood there, grinning like a moron, twirling the carrier around in his hand, with his friends all sniggering, and poor Susan objecting strenuously in her loud Siamese voice. That really infuriated me. I snatched the carrier out of his hand. He made some smart comment and tried to grab one of the dogs. The umbrella was handy. So I—er—tapped his hand with it. Anyway, he got the point. Obviously the story has traveled."

"That's why they call you the Wicked Witch, and because of the hat and your saying you'd put the evil eye on him. Did you really say that?"

"Yes. Somehow it sounds much more lurid now than it seemed at the time."

"Well, Eric is an awful show-off. He often tries to push around some of the younger kids."

"In that case, I'm sorry I didn't put the evil eye on him."

I giggled a little. She smiled. Then I turned back to the pictures. There was another group, this time of a white cat with bluish ears and nose.

"Is this for a book about a Siamese cat?" I asked.

"Yes. I used Susan for a model. She's a lavender point. There she is over on the window seat, sitting on the blue cushion."

I glanced over and looked into a pair of very blue eyes, slightly crossed. "Her eyes are crossed."

"Almost all Siamese cats' eyes are crossed."

"They look funny."

"They probably think you look funny."

I shrugged, and wondered why I always seem to get mixed up with people who are nuts about animals.

"I take it you don't think much of animals."

"They're okay. We have a dog at home. I just don't see why people go bananas over them." I glanced around. "I thought you were supposed to have lots of dogs. All I see is the black one."

"People exaggerate, you know. There were only two others, and before I came to the island I made arrangements to give them to friends near here. They were strays in need of a home. That's why I brought them up." She paused. "Who does the dog you have at home belong to?"

"My brother, Andy. He says Ruggles—that's the dog, a retriever—is his favorite person." I hadn't really meant to say that. It just popped out.

"You like Andy a lot, don't you?"

"Yes."

There was a bit of silence. I started to look at the pictures that were in frames on the floor. They were different from the others—heavier, the colors thicker. They were of the sea, or of the Maine landscape, and somehow seemed sad and lonely. But some of them were of people's heads or of animals. There was one of a dog with a pointed face and long, black silky hair. Then I saw one of a dog that could have been Ruggles. I bent down and picked it up. "This looks like Ruggles," I said. I put it down. The people were interesting. They were nearly all children. And they looked very real. "Are these for books, too?"

"No. I sometimes do portraits. People commission me to do one of their children."

"They pay you?"

"That's right. That's the way I make my living. That, and doing children's books."

"Are you married?"

"Yes. My husband is away for this month. That's why I came up here to paint."

23

"Well—" I looked at my watch. "I have to go now. Marianne will be waiting for me. We have to go to the mainland to do some errands for Granny and have a soda."

"That doesn't sound like—" she started, and then stopped.

I looked quickly at her. "What were you going to say?"

She gave that funny half-smile again. "Just that that didn't sound like your grandmother. She hated all artificial sweets."

"You must know her pretty well."

"I used to. Once."

"Yes. That's what Granny said."

It was pretty boring, I thought. I'd expected the Wicked Witch to be something exciting. Something that Marianne's mother would really disapprove of. Mrs. O'Byrnne was beautiful but ordinary. There wasn't anything really scary about her.

If there wasn't anything really scary about her, I thought, pretending to look over the pictures again, then why did I feel so funny? Like I wanted to get away. I didn't like Mrs. O'Byrnne. I had to admit her pictures were okay, and her house was pretty nice. But she made me want to be somewhere else.

"I have to go now," I said again. "Thanks for showing me the pictures. They're pretty good." I walked across the room and was about to go out, when the big black Lab came over and started sniffing me. I stood still.

"Why don't you call him off?" I said. I didn't want her to see how scared I was. But all of a sudden I started to sweat and I wanted to go to the bathroom.

"All right. Here, Jason. Come back."

Jason, who'd been sort of sniffing the air around me

with his nose up, turned and loped back towards Mrs. O'Byrnne.

"Can I use your bathroom?" I said. I didn't think I could get as far as Marianne's house.

"Of course. It's the second door there."

While I was in the bathroom I made up my mind that, no matter what Jason did, I was going to walk straight across the room and out the door as though he weren't there.

I opened the door. Jason was sitting right in front of it. He was huge. His head seemed to come right up to my chest. "Wuff," he said.

"He's only trying to play, Cathy," Mrs. O'Byrnne said.

"Rrrrrffffff," Jason said again.

I just stood there and concentrated on not showing how I felt.

"Jason, come here," she said sternly. He turned and ran back.

I walked to the door. "Good-bye." I was annoyed. She didn't have to let that big animal come up and sit in front of the bathroom door when I was inside.

"Cathy, just a minute. I have something to ask you." I was right at the door, but I turned. "What?"

"I have another book I'm supposed to illustrate this summer. It's about an eleven-year-old girl. I'd like to use you as a model."

A model. It sounded exciting. Almost like a movie star or the kind of model you see in commercials. But I still thought she shouldn't have let Jason sit in front of the bathroom door. If I was here, being a model for her book, there was no telling what Jason would do. "No, thanks," I said. "I'm pretty busy during the summer."

"You don't want the money?"

"What money?"

I am always broke and had recently asked Daddy for a raise in my allowance, but he had said I didn't need a raise right now. And anyway, he had asked, what did I want the money for? I wanted the money for a bicycle, but I was afraid if I came out and said so, he'd be doubly sure not to give it to me. Daddy and I had already had an argument about a bicycle for me.

"The model's fee," Mrs. O'Byrnne said now. "Models sometimes get paid, you know."

"How much?"

She hesitated. "Two dollars an hour."

I started doing sums in my head. If I got two dollars an hour, how many hours would it take to buy the bicycle I wanted, which cost one hundred and twenty-five dollars? Two into twelve went six times. Two into five went two and a half times. That meant sixty-two and a half hours. "That's sixty-two and a half hours," I said aloud.

"What is it you want one hundred and twenty-five dollars for?"

She was, I had to admit, pretty quick. I started to answer, and then thought that since she was a grown-up, she might have the same ideas as Daddy.

"Just something. . . . Okay, why don't I come and spend . . . two days and nights . . ." I paused. That would only be forty-eight hours. I needed at least twelve more hours. ". . . Three days and two nights." That would be sixty hours. Almost enough. "We'd get it all done at once. And I wouldn't have to come back."

"And what would we do for sleep?"

I just stared at her. I'd completely forgotten about sleep.

"Besides," Mrs. O'Byrnne said, "even with time out for sleep, I couldn't work that way. And you couldn't pose for twelve or fifteen continuous hours." She smiled again. "You may be surprised to find one hour at a stretch a little difficult. Why don't you come for two hours a day for thirty days?"

"That's practically the whole summer," I said.

"No. Only about a month. Take it or leave it."

"How about five dollars?"

"You must come from a long line of New England traders."

"Granny does. So I guess I do, too. How about it?"

"No. I want you here at least two hours a day for a month—or near it. I'll pay two-fifty an hour if you'll come for two hours a day for twenty-five days. That's your one hundred and twenty-five dollars. And if you're faithful—really faithful—about it, I'll . . . I'll give you a bonus at the end."

"How much?"

"I'm not going to tell you that now."

"Well, I think it's pretty unfair. Your idea of a bonus might be fifty cents."

"Do you always argue?"

"Yes."

"Plus ça change."

"What's that?"

"Nothing. It's French—just an expression."

"I know it's French. We have French at school."

"Well, my idea of a bonus is not fifty cents. You're going to have to take some things on trust."

That was something I did not like at all. "I don't like trust. It usually means somebody's trying to put one over on you."

"Who?" she added quickly. "Your mother?"

The words stuck for a minute. Then I thought of Laura. "No. But I think you ought to tell me."

She sighed. "What about twenty dollars? Does that satisfy you?"

Jason had come back and was sitting in front of me, his ears up. "Rrrrrfffff!"

Twenty dollars, I thought. I could put that in the bank and have a running-away fund, in case I ever needed it. "Okay. But you've got to keep Jason away from me."

"All right. I'll see you at ten tomorrow morning."

It was not at all the arrangement I would have liked, but one hundred and twenty-five dollars, plus twenty dollars, was a hundred and forty-five dollars. Somehow that sounded larger than one bicycle plus twenty dollars. Suppose, I thought, running down the path, that instead of getting my top favorite bicycle, I buy the one I saw that was almost as good, but was on sale for only ninety-seven dollars and ninety-eight cents? That would leave me . . . I spent the whole time going down to the Proudy's trying to figure that out to the cent. But every time I tried to visualize the arithmetic, the figures would slide away.

"How much is one hundred and forty-five minus ninety-seven dollars and ninety-eight cents?" I asked Marianne, who was standing by the gate. The funny thing about Marianne is that she's not that bright about a lot of things, but she's a whiz at mental arithmetic.

"Forty-seven dollars and two cents. Why?"

"TerRIFic," I said. That made my emergency fund much larger.

"Why?"

"Oh, nothing. Just doing some mental arithmetic."

"I've been waiting for you for hours. Your grandmother phoned and said we're going over to the mainland. What took you so long?"

I was going to tell her about my visit to the Wicked Witch, but just suddenly I decided not to. Maybe it was the one hundred and forty-five dollars. I'd tell her after I got it.

"Oh, I dawdled," I said. "Come on, let's go."

"How was your afternoon?" Granny asked me, as I gave her the two books the librarian had been saving for her.

"Great! Thanks for the soda." I added, "Marianne said thanks, too."

"As you well know, I don't approve of your eating all that sugar and developing a taste for it. However, . . . I suppose occasionally won't hurt." Her dark eyes looked me up and down. "So you didn't do as Alice asked and change your shirt."

"I brushed this off. It didn't look so bad then. It seemed a pity for Alice to go to all that trouble when it wasn't so dirty."

Granny put down the magazine she was reading. "Cathy, I can just about put up with your being disobedient and defiant. I wasn't any saint myself when I was your age. But I will not have phoniness."

"How am I phony?" I asked indignantly, knowing exactly what she was talking about.

"By pretending to worry over whether or not Alice has too much to do. You wore that shirt because you wanted to. I wish that at the time you bought it, or somebody bought it for you, you had decided to buy two. At least you could have one washed while wearing the other.

As it is, you wear it until it is practically able to stand up by itself."

"I'll take it off now, if you like," I said.

"Yes, I do like. Go upstairs and take it off and bring it down to Alice. We can have dinner then."

I hadn't planned to tell Granny about visiting the Wicked Witch. On the other hand, I hadn't taken a mental vow not to. So when I came back downstairs and went in to dinner, I didn't really know what I was going to do about it. There was no particular reason why I shouldn't tell Granny. She hadn't forbidden me to go there. And Granny, who had said she'd known the Wicked W. for a long time, could answer questions I had about her, such as . . . The funny part was that, although I was intensely curious about the woman painter, I couldn't think of the kind of questions that usually burn a hole in my mind: Does she have any children? Why is she living here by herself? Where does she live during the winter? It wasn't that I wasn't interested. I could easily ask her those questions myself while she was painting me. But my curiosity was about things I had a hard time pinning down. Things like . . .

"You haven't opened your mouth for the entire dinner, Cathy. Are you all right?"

I looked down at my plate, which had started out with vegetables, potatoes and chicken. Now there was nothing on it but a little gravy and a few bones. Evidently I had eaten the entire meal in a trance.

"I'm fine," I said, and shaped the words in my mouth, *This afternoon I went to see the Wicked Witch.* But nothing came out. Instead, I saw the woman's face, beautiful and sad, as though it were right in front of me, and something funny happened in my chest, like a hiccough.

"Catherine, that's the third time I've asked you if you'd like some fruit."

"No, thanks, I'm not hungry," I said quickly.

"What's the matter with you?"

"I guess I'm tired."

"You've never been tired since I've known you."

"Marianne and I did a lot this afternoon."

"Other than go over on the ferry, pick up my books, bring back some groceries and have ice cream sodas, what did you do?"

"Oh, we walked around. Granny, may I be excused? I think I'll go to bed." The moment I said it, I knew it was a mistake. Something else I've never done in my life is go to bed without protest. "But first I'll watch some television."

Granny, who had been looking at me in a probing way, seemed to relax. She doesn't really approve of television either—at least she doesn't approve of the programs that I like to watch. But she knows I always like the tube and she had, in fact, rented the set now in her living room when she found out I was going to be up here without the family.

"Okay. Are you sure you feel all right? You don't have a sore throat?"

"No, Granny. I feel fine. I'll just go and watch 'The Little House on the Prairie.' "

She sighed. "There must be something to be said for television, but right at the moment I can't think what it is."

I really didn't particularly want to watch television. I wanted to go to my room and think. But I knew if I did that, Granny would think something funny was going on. So I sat and watched a couple of shows and thought

31

about the next morning, and all the mornings to come for twenty-five days. I knew I'd have to make up something to tell Granny and Marianne, and I didn't know what it would be, but decided I'd worry about it the next day. The one thing I never considered was telling them about the Wicked Witch and my pact with her to pose as a model.

three

I was running around and around the edge of a black hole and trying desperately to run faster and faster, because I knew that if I slowed, I'd not only fall into the black pit beneath me, but whatever or whoever was chasing me would catch me. Just as I thought my lungs would burst, I woke up. There was a smell of coffee wafting through the house and Granny was calling me.

"Cathy? Are you awake?"

I glanced at my bedside clock and couldn't believe it was nearly eight o'clock. Usually I wake up around six-thirty.

"Coming," I yelled, and threw back the covers. I'd taken a bath the night before, so it didn't take me long to brush my teeth and put on my jeans and sweat shirt. If I'd had my Big Apple sweat shirt, I would have put it on, dirt and all, to make me feel better. But Alice probably had it in the washing machine by now, so I put another one on that said I'M A TEENAGE SEX MANIAC on the front. Granny hadn't seen that, and I thought it would give me courage.

As I walked into the dining room Granny took one look at the words across my front and closed her eyes. "There are times," she said, "when I feel that mass literacy may be a mistake."

"What's mass literacy?" I asked, sliding into my seat and reaching for the cereal box.

"It means that people like you with no judgment and even less taste can read and wear slogans such as that monstrosity all over your chest."

"You noticed," I said, feeling better already.

"Wasn't that the whole idea? Here's the milk." She passed the pitcher to me. "I suppose one should feel thankful for all mercies, however small."

I looked at her over my cornflakes and milk. "What mercies?" I said, blowing out a spray of milk.

"It's always better not to talk with your mouth full."

"Sorry."

"The mercy I had in mind was that, with that legend printed over your front, it's just as well you're still flat as a board."

"I am *not*," I said, and pushed out my chest. "See?"

She sighed. "No offense."

I stared down at my two almost invisible blips. One of the things that annoys me is that Marianne, who is three months younger and smaller and dumber, has bigger blips. "They'll grow," I said. "Anyway, it's tacky to have a big bozoom now."

"I hope you don't live to eat those words," Granny said. "There's no telling what you'll develop."

A few minutes later I got up from the table, thinking that maybe, if I did it quietly and before Granny was thinking, she'd forget to ask what I was going to do.

"What are you and Marianne going to do today?"

"Oh, just hang around, I guess."

Granny opened her mouth, as though she were going to say something, then closed it. "Don't forget," she said finally. "Lunch at one."

This time, without being asked, I took my sweater.

* * *

Jason came baying down the path. I stood still. "Come on, Jason, you know me." I tried to sound full of confidence. He came and sniffed around, then nearly gave me a heart attack by rearing up on his hind legs and putting his paws on my shoulders. Standing on his hind legs, he was as tall as I was. Then he licked my face.

"Don't do that!" I pushed him off. He looked wounded.

When I got in, I saw that the Wicked Witch had been watching from the window. "You hurt his feelings," she said.

"Well, I don't like having my face slobbered over."

"There are a lot worse things than a big wet kiss from a nice dog."

"Like what?"

She looked at me for a minute. "Like not having a big wet kiss from a nice dog."

"Where would you like me to pose?"

"You can go and sit on that window seat to begin with."

One of the few pieces of furniture in the room was a baby grand piano in one corner. She leaned against that, with a big pad in her hand. I went over to the window seat. The Siamese cat, Susan, was there. When I sat down, she raised her head with its crossed blue eyes and yawned. She's really pretty, I thought, with pink edging her ears, like shells with the light shining through. I'd never really had any desire to touch an animal before, but I decided to see if she was as soft as she looked and put out my hand.

Susan pulled her head back, her crossed eyes staring fixedly at me.

A little annoyed, I thrust my hand forward to stroke her head. But she sat up and I heard a small hiss. It was plain she wanted no part of me. I was suddenly determined that I was going to stroke her whether she liked it or not.

"Come here," I said, and made a grab at her.

I don't know quite what happened then. There was a squawk, a much louder hiss and the next thing I knew there was a growing red line of blood on my wrist. Susan was crouched a foot away, her ears back, a funny low growl coming from her.

"You scratched me!" I said, furious, and slapped her.

Susan jumped down off the seat and moved towards the door. I could see then that one back leg was shorter than the other.

"Don't *ever* hit an animal," Mrs. O'Byrnne said.

"She scratched me. All I wanted to do was stroke her."

"She doesn't know you, and you moved your hand too fast towards her. After all, from her point of view you're huge and threatening."

I hate to lose my temper. It makes me feel that the other person has power over me, like a tiger over a mouse. But I was angry. "I should think you'd be mad at her, not me. I didn't do anything to her—at least not at first. She started it."

She didn't say anything for a minute. "I didn't mean to sound angry. It . . . it upset me when you struck Susan. She's very dear to me. But I should have remembered . . ."

"I think I'll go home," I said.

Mrs. O'Byrnne didn't say anything. She was looking at me, her eyes level and blue-green like the sea. Finally she said, "No work, no pay."

I was about to tell her that she could keep her pay, when in my imagination I saw that beautiful English bicycle in front of me, like a hanging plant. . . . Andy has a bicycle, which he rides in Central Park. I had asked Daddy why I couldn't have a bicycle if Andy, who is only a year and a half older, was allowed to have one.

"For one thing, Cathy, I didn't buy it for him. His uncle—Laura's brother—did. For another, when I ask Andy not to ride it in the streets or on the sidewalk, he does what I ask. You and I both know you wouldn't."

"That's not fair," I said.

"Why isn't it fair?"

"Because you're different to him than you are to me."

"If I am, it's because I'm basing that difference on your own behavior. You have to take responsibility for what you do, and part of that includes, sometimes, the way people react when you provoke them."

I carefully didn't speak to Daddy after that for three days. He didn't seem to pay any attention, but Laura did. On the third day, out of the blue, she said to me, "Cathy, if you truly promise that you won't ride your bicycle in the streets, that you'll take it to the park and ride there with Andy, then I'll see if your father will change his ruling about getting you a bike."

"It's not fair," I said again.

"From your father's viewpoint it is. You know that you often break a rule just for the sake of breaking it. And his rule about the bicycle is for your own and other people's safety."

We didn't say anything for a minute. Laura went on putting dishes in the dishwasher. When she put in the last plate, she looked at me and said, "Well, do you promise?"

I was furious. "What's the point of having a bike if I just have a bunch of rules to go with it?"

"It's up to you. You give me your promise, and I'll talk to your father."

But I wanted a bicycle without the rules. I hadn't thought of it before, but when the Wicked Witch offered to pay me for modeling, it suddenly burst on me that if I bought the bicycle with my own money, then I wouldn't have to have anybody's rules but my own. Which was the reason for my agreeing to come up every day to the Wicked Witch's cottage in the first place.

I didn't want Mrs. O'Byrnne to think I was giving in, so I didn't reply to her "no work, no pay." I just sat and stared out the window. I also found I was thinking about the cat, Susan, and the funny way she walked. I suppose, I thought, if something as big as I am to Susan came rushing up to me and stuck out an arm, then I'd be watching out for my rights, too. I wondered if I'd hurt her when I slapped her and found that I was hoping very much that I hadn't. It wasn't a hard slap . . .

"What happened to Susan's leg?" I asked suddenly.

"She was born with some kind of bone problem. Her back legs were never too steady. And then she fell once and damaged one of her legs so that it had to be operated on."

I stared out the window. Susan had gone outside and was sitting up, washing one of her paws. Next to her, watching, was Jason. Beyond them over the edge of the cliff was the sea. Right now the sun was on it, so that it looked blue-green, like Mrs. O'Byrnne's eyes. Birds were twittering around the window and flying across the front of the house in great swoops.

"Doesn't Susan try and catch the birds?" I asked.

"No. She knows that she can't move fast enough for that, so she pretends to ignore them."

A sort of silence started. It was strange. I'd never before thought of a time when nobody spoke as *silence*. To me it had always been a piece of time when people were thinking of something to say or how to answer something that somebody else had said.

But that morning, and for all the other mornings I was with her, sitting on the window seat or on the floor or occasionally outside, I came to think of my time there as a river of silence that just flowed with islands of talk. At first it was uncomfortable, but after a while I liked it. Which didn't mean that we didn't say anything at all. It just meant that I wasn't nervous when we didn't, and as time passed I knew it wasn't because she was angry or was about to spring something on me.

After I'd been sitting there for a while that morning, I said, "Doesn't your husband like it up here?"

"My husband works for a newspaper and has been sent to the Middle East to do a story."

"Oh. Do you have any children?"

She didn't answer at first, then she said, "My husband has children by his first marriage. They stay with us sometimes."

All the time she spoke she went on drawing, turning a page after she'd finished with it. She'd look at me for a while, then draw something. Or she'd walk around and look at me from another angle.

"How many children's books have you made pictures for?" I asked her at one point.

"Three."

"That's not a lot." After all, she was at least forty.

"I started late. Turn your head a little, towards the window."

"Do you like doing it?"

"Yes. Very much."

She drew for a while in silence. Then she said, "Where do you go to school, Cathy?"

"To Beresford School." Beresford is a school in New York.

"Do you like it?"

"Not especially."

"That's too bad, considering how much time you have to spend there."

I shrugged and said nothing. Talking about school is boring.

There was another long silence, then I said, "What do you want me to call you?" I didn't really know why I asked that, except that I had a hard time using a name when I thought of her, and I couldn't keep calling her the Wicked Witch, even to myself, because it was so silly.

"You can call me Elizabeth, if you like."

Somehow it didn't feel right. "I never call a grown-up by a first name."

"What about your stepmother?"

It was true. I did call Laura, Laura. "That's different," I said.

"Why?" She lowered her pad and looked at me.

"Well, she's an almost mother."

"I see." She raised the pad again and drew some more. "Well, then, you decide. What would you like to call me?"

I thought about *Aunt* Elizabeth. But she wasn't my aunt, so it would be a pretend thing and I didn't like pretend things. "I guess I'll call you Elizabeth."

She smiled then. She'd moved so that the sun was on her face, and I could see that her hair was not really mouse-colored. It was blonde with gray and white in it, which made it look mousey in ordinary light. But now it looked a silvery gold. She had wide cheekbones and a squarish chin and long hands with thin fingers. Every detail seemed clear and important, as though she were out of a storybook, like a princess or a queen. My heart gave the funny, odd hiccough that it had given before.

"I guess that'll be all this morning," she said.

She moved then, so that she was out of the sun. The golden look was gone, and her face just looked tired.

I looked at my watch. It was only eleven-thirty. So that I hadn't stayed the full two hours. If I left now, after only an hour and a half, I wondered if she would cut down the bonus. I was standing in the middle of the room, thinking about this and trying to figure how I was going to say something about it, when she said, "Don't worry. This won't cut short your bonus."

"How did you know I was thinking about that?"

Her lips curved up. "I could almost hear the click of that calculator in your head, the one that seems to be going most of the time."

"Well, when you want something very much and the only way you're going to get it is to save, then you have to work out how much you're going to need," I said.

"True. I suppose you're still not going to tell me what it is."

"It's a bicycle," I said.

"Does your father know you're saving up for this?"

"Daddy won't let me have it. Even though Andy has one."

"Andy. He's your stepbrother, isn't he?"

I frowned. "I don't think of him as *step*. He's just my brother." I was irritated as I always am when somebody makes this distinction.

"I see. You mean . . . How did he happen to get his bicycle?"

"His uncle gave it to him. The one I want is even better than his. It's English, with ten speeds. His has only three."

She picked up the pad and made a long, sweeping line on it with her pencil. "Is there some reason why your father won't let you have a bicycle when your st— your brother has one?"

Just thinking about it made me angry. "If you've finished drawing me, I have to go now," I said.

"Did I make you angry?"

I shrugged. "Like I said, I have to go."

Then she did something that knocked me flat. She put down her pad, came over, put her hands on my shoulders and kissed me on the cheek. "I'm sorry. I should mind my own business."

I knew if I stayed another two minutes she'd see me cry. And I never like people seeing me cry.

"Good-bye," I said, and walked out as quickly as I could without looking as though I was rushing.

"Where've you been?" Marianne asked. "I've been waiting around for *hours*."

"I went for a walk."

"A *walk*. I thought we'd go down to the pier and watch the boats."

"I'm bored with that."

"What else is there to do?"

That was the trouble. There wasn't much else, except maybe to go and take lessons at Miss Ashford's riding school. "I was thinking of taking riding lessons," I said.

"Great! I'll ask Mother if I can, too. She said last summer she thought I could this year."

My heart sank. I wanted to keep my visits to Elizabeth O'Byrnne's house a secret from both Marianne and Granny. But I was beginning to see that it was going to be extremely difficult. And then I had an inspiration. "The trouble is, Marianne, I had a letter from my parents, who'd heard from my school. The school wants to put me back a year because my grades are so awful. But Laura and Daddy say that if I work this summer—at least during the mornings—then maybe they won't put me back."

Marianne stared at me in wonder. "You never said a word about this. I thought you got nothing but A's and B's. In fact, you said you did."

I had said it, and it was true. "I guess that was what I thought and I was wrong. Anyway, Granny has outlined some reading for me to do and we're going to work together on it during the mornings."

"That's terrible. I mean, I have a reading list, too, and it's pretty awful to have to get through it. But nobody really lowers the boom on me about it. You like to read, so maybe you won't hate it. But I don't know what I'm supposed to do in the mornings now. All the other kids around here are about sixteen or practically in kindergarten."

I knew that sooner or later I might have to do a lot of explaining, and I'd probably get Granny's annual lecture on being truthful and not lying. But I also knew that Granny didn't think too much of Mrs. Proudy and didn't talk to her very often. So maybe, at least for the next twenty-five days, Granny wouldn't get any feedback from her about my having to work in the mornings.

After that . . . well, after that, I'd just have to see.

It was strange, but all the time I was thinking this, I was also thinking how funny it was how much I wanted no one to know about my going to see the Wicked W. (Somehow it still seemed easier for me to think of her as the Wicked W. than as Elizabeth.) It was as though the most important thing in my life right now was that my going to see her be a secret. I glanced at Marianne and decided that I had to do everything I could to make sure she wouldn't call up some morning and say (to Granny or Alice) that she hated to interrupt my morning studies, but . . .

"And Granny is absolutely *fanatic* about my not being interrupted," I said. "She seems to think that one measly little phone call will ruin a whole morning's work."

"Well, I'd better not call then." Marianne was as obedient as ever. "But you'll be sure to call me the minute you're through, won't you?"

"Of course I will," I said.

"But then, when are you taking riding lessons?"

Why did I mention riding? I thought with irritation. Now I'd have to do something about it or backtrack in some way.

Marianne was still on the subject. "Maybe we could do it after lunch," she said.

"Well, now that I think about it, I'm not sure it's such a good idea."

"Why not? I think it's terrific. I like horses, don't you?"

Animals again. Andy rides in New York every Saturday morning. Daddy had offered to let me take lessons, too. But horses are not only animals, they are much bigger than I am. Why did I even mention it? The answer was that it was the only thing I could think of at the moment when I was looking for an explanation for something that would keep me busy during the mornings. That was before I thought of having to do schoolwork.

"We'll see," I said, as vague as possible, hoping she'd forget about it.

Telling Granny what I was doing was, for the moment, no problem. She just assumed that I was with Marianne. Also, I knew it was against her principles to fuss too much. Once she had said to me, "I don't like overprotective parents, grandparents, or adults, in general, Cathy. I go on the theory that by eleven you should have some sense of responsibility for yourself, and that you won't abuse my trust." Then she turned her probing dark eyes on me. "Am I right?"

"Absolutely," I said, and tried not to squirm. When Daddy's around, he really wants to know all the time where I'm going and what I'm doing, and I've become pretty good at giving him the kind of answer that doesn't tell him too much, but isn't vague enough to make him suspicious. For instance, on a Saturday afternoon when he asks where I'm going, I tell him I'm going to Janet's house, but I don't tell him I'm going to stop by the bicycle shop on the way.

So the following morning I slipped out of my seat at the breakfast table and said to Granny, "See you at lunch."

Granny lowered her copy of *The New York Times*. This time I had brought my cardigan down to breakfast and was putting it on over my sweat shirt without being told.

"Have a pleasant morning," Granny said. She looked as though she might say something else, so I left quickly.

* * *

And for a while everything went smoothly. Nobody asked me what I was doing, and Marianne only referred to the riding lessons every second or third day.

I'd go up to the Wicked W.'s house and sit, or walk around or stand, while she drew page after page of sketches. Sometimes I'd just sit there on the window seat and stare out at the sea. In some way I couldn't quite put my finger on, she wasn't like any grown-up I'd ever known. It wasn't that she didn't ask me questions, a habit grown-ups have. But the questions seemed different, and she waited to see what I would say, as though it were terribly important, and not just to see if I was doing something wrong, or forbidden or disapproved of.

"What do you like to do best?" she asked one morning.

I immediately thought of Andy, as though he were right outside the window, looking in, the sun on his red hair.

"I dunno. Be with Andy, I guess." I went on staring out the window, imagining Andy there, in his jeans and shirt, beckoning me to come down and play on the beach. But then—it was almost as though, instead of imagining it, I was watching a movie—a big gold dog ran up and jumped around Andy. Andy stopped looking in the window at me, and started throwing a stick for Ruggles to retrieve. Then he started down the path, Ruggles leaping ahead.

But it was just imagining. Andy wasn't outside. He was off at a camp, and Ruggles was in Connecticut at the farm where he was born, running to the drive every time a car came in, thinking it might be Andy.

"What's the matter, Cathy? You look unhappy."

"Nothing," I said.

46

"Then unclench your fists."

I looked down at my hands. I bite my nails some-times, so they're short and look nibbled, but they were dug into the palms of my hands. As I opened my hands, I could see the crescents they'd made.

"What were you thinking about?"

"I was thinking about Andy."

"What were you thinking about him?" she asked, and sat down beside me. She smelled like a blend of flowers and paint.

"It was like a movie. He was out there, telling me to come down to the beach. Then Ruggles came, and he forgot about me and ran with Ruggles down to the beach without me." I paused. "I know it's not really true. I was just imagining it. But it felt true."

"And it makes you unhappy? That when Ruggles came, he forgot about you? Is that the way it really is?"

I shrugged. "He likes Ruggles better than he does me. He told me so."

She didn't say anything for a minute. Then she got up. "I guess we have to accept the fact that we can't be first with everybody all the time."

I had another dream that night. Again I was running away. I was running down a hall with many doors, but every time I tried to open one, it was locked. So I went on running, because somebody was running after me. Finally, there was a door at the end of the hall, and I tore towards it and jerked the handle. But it also was locked and I was trapped. I turned, waiting to see who it was running down the hall towards me. Just as she was about to come under the light so I could see her, the door behind me opened suddenly, and I fell through. But, just before I fell, I had a quick flash of blue, a face, red and violent, and hair like straw sticking out of a head. I screamed and screamed.

"Cathy, Cathy, wake up! Wake up!" My grandmother in her red robe was sitting on the bed beside me, shaking me by the shoulder.

"Granny!" I cried, and sat up and put my arms around her. "Save me!"

"Good heavens," Granny said, putting her arms around me and holding me tight. "You sound like something out of a revival meeting. What do you want to be saved from?"

I rested there, my face against her arm. She smelled nice. Like talcum powder. That made me remember the Wicked W., who smelled of paint and flowers.

"She was running after me," I said.

"Who?"

"That monster. A she-monster, with a red face and blue robe and hair made of straw." I was surprised, myself, at how clear she was in my head, although I couldn't see her face.

After a minute Granny said, "You had a bad dream. A nightmare. You had one the other night, only by the time I got to your room, you had evidently slept yourself out of it."

"What time is it?"

"One o'clock."

"It's dark in here."

"Let's put on a light."

Granny got up and turned on the overhead light and two lamps. My windows were open and I could smell the sea outside and hear it sush-sushing against the beach.

"Here," Granny said. She'd gone into my bathroom and come out with my washcloth. "Put this against your temples and wrists." She held it against my temples. I shivered. "It's cold," I said.

"That's right. Now put it on your wrists."

I held it on one wrist and then on another. "I used to do this for you when you were a little child. Remember?"

I shook my head. "No, I don't remember at all. Why did you do it then?"

"You had bad dreams, just the way you have now, so I'd wake you up and put on the light and put cold water on your head and wrists and keep you awake for a while. Then you'd go peacefully back to sleep."

I sat there, shivering, holding the cold wet cloth against my wrists. Even though the light was on, I felt frightened, as though it were dark.

"Now," Granny said. "Do you think you can go to sleep if I turn out the light?"

"No. Please don't go." I stared at her. "Why don't you lie down on the bed beside me? You could put the quilt over you."

"Thank you," Granny said dryly. "Your bed is a little small for an adult body, let alone an adult and a half."

"You mean I'm a half?"

"I do. You're an important half. But you're a half." She smiled at me for a minute. "My bed is bigger. Would you like to come in and get in beside me?"

Even though I like to be very independent and don't like people to think that I can't be alone, I said yes very quickly.

She got up. "All right, come on."

"I think I'll go to the bathroom first."

"All right. Then come on down the hall."

Just before I left to go to Granny's room, I took Jocko with me. Jocko is a stuffed monkey that somebody gave me a long time ago, I'm not sure who. He's quite big, about a third as big as I am now, one ear is badly torn and he's dirty. But there are times when he's terribly important.

Granny's room is larger than mine, with windows facing the ocean and others, along the side, facing north to the Nova Scotia coastline. I went over to the window and looked out. There was a small bright moon that left a trail in the water underneath. The shore was black, but the sky was almost light. Just suddenly I wished I was home in our New York apartment on the West Side, with people yelling in the street beneath and sirens sounding and sometimes, in hot weather, a funny rotting smell coming from garbage that has not been collected.

"I wish I was in New York," I said.

"Come to bed, Cathy," Granny said.

I turned. "I brought Jocko. I thought he could come to bed with us."

Granny looked at me over the covers. "They say that three's company, but bring him along. It's good I have a queen-sized bed. I thought I was being self-indulgent to keep it after your grandfather died, but I see now that there was a Purpose for it." I could tell by the way she said "Purpose" that it had a capital P.

I climbed into bed next to Granny and put Jocko on the outside.

"Everything all right now, Cathy?"

"Fine," I said. It was funny how much better I felt in Granny's room, lying next to her in bed.

Granny turned out the light and slid down under the covers. I backed into her, so that my back and fanny were against her side. Then I put my arms around Jocko.

I wanted, suddenly, to tell Granny that I was going every morning up to the Wicked W.'s to model. In fact, I wanted to tell her so much that I could feel the words, like soft marbles, on my tongue. But then I saw the bicycle, as though it were hanging in the air, its wheels slowly going around. After that I saw myself on it, riding like the wind around the roads in Central Park, Jocko on the back, having a race with Andy and winning by miles.

"Of course," I said to Andy, still in my imagination, when he finally came up to the starting place at the Ninetieth Street entrance, "I have a much better bike."

"What did you say?" Granny asked.

I was not going to tell her about the Wicked W., I decided. If I told her, I couldn't go back. "Please sing me something, Granny," I said. "Something sleepy."

She sighed. "Maybe if I do, it will put me to sleep, too. All right, here goes." And she hummed something that was slow and kind of sweet.

"What's its name?" I asked.

"Well, sometimes it's called 'Humoresque,' and sometimes it's called 'Passengers Will Please Refrain.' "

"Refrain from what?"

"It's a joke. Go to sleep."

four

" 'Passengers Will Please Refrain' from what?" I repeated the next morning at breakfast.

"Your generation is really too young for the joke," Granny said, pouring me out some milk. "You travel on buses, planes and in cars, not in trains, which is a shame. Trains are—were—wonderful. Anyway, in the toilets on trains there always used to be a sign that said, 'Passengers will please refrain from flushing toilets while the train is in the station.' "

"Why? What's so bad about that?"

"Use your considerable imagination, Cathy. The flushing mechanism was not the chemical toilet that you have now in planes, trains and buses. Nor was it the involved sewer pipe affair you have in stationary bathrooms in houses. It was simply a trapdoor. When you pulled the chain, everything fell out straight to the ground. If this happened in the station, it would have been . . . er . . . unaesthetic."

I thought about it. "I see. But what's that got to do with the tune you sang?"

"Some wit found that the words to the notice fit the tune of 'Humoresque' which was often played by orchestras in hotel lounges during tea at the time when everybody traveled everywhere by train."

"It doesn't seem that funny."

"After all that explanation, nothing would seem funny."

52

I nibbled at an English muffin. "That must have been a long time ago."

"Back in the Middle Ages, when I was young."

I grinned at Granny. "Ha, ha."

She smiled back at me. "How do you feel?"

"Fine." I ate some more muffin. "I liked last night. I mean, after I came into your room." It was true, just thinking about going to sleep with my back next to Granny made me feel good.

"Well, you have an open invitation. And you're the only living creature that I would say that to."

"You mean, because Grandfather is dead."

Granny poured herself some more coffee. "Well, yes. But I was also thinking about Pocketa, who died last summer."

"Your Siamese cat?"

"That's right. In warm weather she'd sleep curled up in the middle of my back. In cold weather she'd get under the covers with me."

I had forgotten about Pocketa. And then, before I knew what I was saying, I said, "I met a Siamese cat the other day. It was lame."

"Oh? Where?"

By that time I remembered that she didn't know about my visit to Elizabeth. "In the village. On the mainland," I lied.

Granny looked at me for a minute. "I thought I knew all the cats in the village. Certainly all the Siamese. Where did you see this one?"

"Oh, just walking along."

"How lame?"

"One leg was a bit stiff, that's all. Can I be excused?"

"You haven't finished your muffin."

"I'm not hungry."

Granny sighed. I was suddenly quite sure she knew I was lying. "All right. You're excused."

When I got to Elizabeth's house, I saw Susan on her seat underneath the window. Susan and I had pretty much left each other alone since the scratching incident. Often she'd leave the room when I came in, jumping out a window or slipping into the bedroom. This time, though, she didn't move. Maybe, I thought, she's forgotten our spat. I started over. Susan got up, arched her back, jumped down from the window seat and marched away, her uneven leg making her walk de-*dum*, de-*dum*.

"Never mind," Elizabeth said. "It takes awhile."

"She doesn't like me."

"Well, you did slap her."

"She scratched me first."

"I told you, sticking your hand out was to her a threatening gesture. But give her time. When she comes back in, hold out your hand and call her. She may come over."

"I don't care. She's just a cat. Where do you want me to sit?"

"I want you to stand and lean out the window, as though you were watching for someone. And talk to me while you're doing that."

"What shall I talk about?"

"You live here with your grandmother, don't you?"

"Yes."

Susan was outside with Jason. Jason had barked when I came up, and then did his act with his paws on my shoulders, licking my face with his tongue. I decided that I rather liked his greeting me that way. It showed he appreciated me. Now he was lying, sound asleep, on the grass between the house and the rocky cliffs and trees. Susan was sitting in front of him, patting his face with her paw. As I watched, she stopped doing that and leaned over and started to lick his fur. "Susan's licking Jason," I said.

Elizabeth glanced out the window and smiled. "Sometimes I think she thinks he's one of her kittens, grown to an impossible size."

"Granny had a Siamese," I said. "She was named Pocketa."

"Yes, I remember Pocketa."

I turned. "You do? Granny said Pocketa always slept with her."

"That's right. Pocketa used to lie next to your grandmother's back."

"You must have known Granny very well."

"I did."

I waited for her to say something else about it. But she didn't.

"I slept with Granny last night. It was nice. That's when she told me about Pocketa."

Elizabeth looked at me. "Do you always sleep with your grandmother?"

"No. I had a nightmare. I guess I must have made a noise, because she woke me up with a wet cloth at my wrists and forehead. Then she said I could sleep with her."

"I remember—" She suddenly caught her breath, as though she had hiccoughed.

"What?"

"Nothing. Wet cloths used to be an old cure for nightmares. What did you dream?"

"Somebody was chasing me. A woman in a blue robe with hair like a mess of straw. She had a red face, but I couldn't see what it looked like. I mean, I'm not sure I'd know her."

"Have you had this dream before?"

"Yes. About a week ago." I said suddenly, "I hate it. It's like it really happened."

We didn't say anything for a bit. She drew and I stared out the window at Susan and Jason. After a while I said, "That's a funny name for a cat, Pocketa. I wonder what it means."

"It's the sound your heart makes. If you listened to it through a stethoscope or some other amplifying device, you'd hear it thumping away, going *pock*eta, *pock*eta, *pock*eta, *pock*eta."

"But why name a cat that?"

"Your father—"

I turned. "You knew my father?"

"Yes. A long time ago."

"Do you know Laura?"

"No, I never met her. By the way, you've mentioned your grandmother, your father and Laura, your stepmother. You've never mentioned your mother."

"She's dead."

"I see." Elizabeth drew for a while. Then she said, "Move over to that seat, will you, so that the sun is on your face, and turn towards me. All right," she said, when I had done as she told me, and was sitting, both feet on the floor, facing her. "When did your mother die?"

"When I was five."

"Do you remember her?"

"Not exactly."

"What do you mean, 'not exactly'?"

I wasn't sure what I meant. Sometimes, when I wasn't trying, I almost remembered her. But never so that I could recall her face afterwards. There was something now, at the very edge of my mind. I couldn't quite get it.

"Do I have to stay still?" I said. "Can't I walk around?"

"Yes, if you want to. So you don't remember her."

"No."

Jason was now on his back, his four paws in the air, and Susan was slowly, methodically, licking his side.

"Don't you have any pictures of her?"

"No."

I'd never seen a picture of her. For the first time it struck me as strange. I stared out at Susan, licking away. Jason had his eyes closed, his face extended along the ground, as though he were being massaged and finding it blissful.

"Jason looks in heaven."

Elizabeth looked up from her pad, glanced at me and then out at Jason. She smiled. "He is."

I remembered the big black dog, running at me, looking a mile high and making a noise like crunched bones. "But he's so fierce—sometimes."

"Not to people he loves."

He licked my face, I remembered.

"He adores Susan," Elizabeth said. "I think he, too, thinks she's his mother."

"You don't have a doghouse or a basket. Where do they sleep?"

"With me. It makes things a little crowded, but it's nice."

I glanced out again. Susan had worked her way up Jason's chest and was now licking one of his longish ears. I turned back to say something. Elizabeth was watching Susan and Jason, a smile on her mouth, her eyes warm and crinkled, like a mother watching her children, I thought suddenly.

I don't really know quite what happened then, or why I did what I did. But I pushed up the window and leaned out and yelled "Yaaaaaahhhhhh!" as loud as I could.

Susan was a white streak going towards the rocks. She tried to jump up on one and fell back. Jason leapt to his feet and was barking frantically.

Elizabeth stood up. Her cheeks were red. "Why did you do that, Cathy?"

The trouble was, I didn't know. I got up. "I think I'd better go now.

"Yes. No. I don't know. *Why—*?"

I ran out the door. Susan was crouched beneath the rock, her ears back. Jason lunged after me, barking. I knew I ought to stand still, that he would stop barking and lick my face again. But I kept on running. I heard Elizabeth calling him, "Jason, Jason!" After a while he stopped chasing after me and barking and turned back.

When I got down to the beach, I sat there for a while, staring at the sea. Far to the left there were some little kids building a sandcastle. A few feet away from them a woman sat, watching. At the other end of the beach, almost at the tip of the island, Mr. Gunn was mending his boat next to a jetty. Mr. Gunn is old and cross and doesn't like anybody. He doesn't say much. Mostly he grunts. He spends practically all his time out in his boat, fishing. I've always liked him and I decided to go over and talk to him.

"Hi," I said, when I got up to his boat. It was up on the sand. Beside it there was a small pot of hot tar, some canvas strips and an open toolbox.

Mr. Gunn grunted. He was hammering some strips of wood, taking the nails out of his mouth as he went along. Behind him lay MacDuff, his German shepherd, who also is old. He's blackish and tan and gray around his mouth. MacDuff has been the great exception to my feeling about animals. I don't know why, but I've always liked him. Going over, I sat down beside him and put my hands on his fur. He raised his big head and looked at me out of his yellow eyes. Then he put his head down, but his tail thumped the sand.

"Mr. Gunn," I said, "do you ever do things that you don't mean to do, and you don't know why?"

He grunted, took another nail out of his mouth and hammered it.

"Just now I yelled and screamed at a dog and a cat who were lying down—at least the dog was, the cat was licking him—and they weren't doing any harm at all. But I shouted and scared them on purpose. And Elizabeth, the woman who paints, was horrified. She didn't say she was, but I knew. She asked me why I did it, but I couldn't tell her."

Mr. Gunn grunted again and hammered another nail.

I lay down, my side against MacDuff, and stared at the sky. It was as blue as Alice's mixing bowl. There were white clouds that looked like cauliflower heads and gray, white and black triangles—sea gulls—that wheeled and screamed.

After a while the sky, the clouds and the sea gulls all seemed to blur. Peace came over me. Mr. Gunn went on hammering. MacDuff started to snore. I had my left hand over my eyes, with my watch pressing into my forehead. Even though I hadn't checked the time, I knew it was long past twelve. Marianne would be wondering where I was. I had told her that Granny would be upset if she called and interrupted the morning work I had said I was doing. But if it was past twelve, wouldn't she feel free to call? Maybe. Probably. Then she'd discover I wasn't there and there was no morning work and I had lied about the whole thing. Would she stop being my summer best friend? Maybe. Maybe not. Until some more kids came up, it was me or nobody. What would Granny do? She'd know I was lying to Marianne. So then she'd want to know what I was really doing when I said I was at home working . . .

MacDuff gave a sigh. I stroked him for a minute. Mr. Gunn was still hammering. Everything in my life looked as though it were coming unstuck, and all I did was lie there with MacDuff, listening to Mr. Gunn hammering, and staring at the sky. Every now and then this happened to me—what Daddy would call Impending Disaster—with me doing nothing, as though it were all going on with somebody else, somewhere else, and I was on the side, watching.

I went to sleep.

"Lassie, lassie!"

I turned over. Mr. Gunn was staring down at me, his

big boots next to my face. "I'm goin' out for a wee row," he said.

I sat up. "I'll go with you." I had been out with him in his boat several times before, the previous year, and had been told by my father that I was never to do that again. Never. "That pig-headed old man rows his boat straight out into the ocean," Daddy said. "Nobody knows why. So far he's made it home again. But let a storm come up and one day he might not. You're not to go with him again, Cathy. Understand?"

"All right, Daddy."

I wondered why I hadn't argued more. I must have been thinking of a birthday present I wanted him to give me. My birthday is in late June, usually when I'm up here. And I try to be particularly good for at least two weeks before.

"Yer father says yer no can come in the boat," Mr. Gunn said now. He took the pipe out of his mouth and spat into the sand.

"That was ages ago. He wouldn't mind now. Anyway, he isn't here." Just to make sure Mr. Gunn didn't prevent me from going, I jumped into the boat.

"I'll no tak the responsibility," he said.

"Please." I didn't know why I was so anxious to go— apart from the fact that I wasn't supposed to. But I knew suddenly that I did not want to go back to the house. And I didn't want to see Marianne. And I didn't want to go on errands to the mainland. I wanted to be alone. And being with Mr. Gunn and MacDuff was like being alone, only better.

"Please," I said again. "I was just a little kid then. I'm *much* older now." I found all of a sudden that unless

I was really careful, I might cry. I tried hard to think about something funny, to make myself laugh instead . . . something like Alice on roller skates, or . . . or . . . but instead I saw Susan, the Siamese, trying to jump up on the rocks and falling back.

I didn't have a handkerchief. Slowly Mr. Gunn opened his toolbox, got out a roll of paper towels, tore off a piece and handed it to me.

"Yer a bad lassie, tha's for sure," he said, and pushed the boat into the water. "MacDuff!" he suddenly roared. The big dog stood up, shook the sand out of his coat and took a stiff-legged leap into the boat. Mr. Gunn unfolded a huge shawl-like wrap and put it on a big coil of rope in the bottom of the boat. "Sit!" he said to MacDuff.

But MacDuff climbed onto the seat in the back of the boat beside me. I blew my nose in the paper towel, stuck it into my jeans pocket and put my arm around MacDuff. Mr. Gunn rowed straight out into the sea, just the way I wanted him to.

Except for the sound of the water slapping against the boat and the squeaking of the oars in the oarlocks, there was a huge silence. Mr. Gunn was facing us but not looking at us. After a while MacDuff lay with his front paws on my lap, and I stared past Mr. Gunn at the water and the dark green fir trees coming down to the shore. Everything unimportant seemed to hold still while a story unfolded itself in my head . . .

Gunn, MacDuff, Andy and I would row across the sea. We would take bottled water and soda, sandwiches, peanut butter, apples and canned dog food. After a few days, we'd come to a large island that no one had ever discovered before, because most of the time it was mysteriously invisible. Columbus had not only missed it,

everyone else had, too. Even the airplanes overhead never saw it. When we landed, Gunn would take it in the name of Queen Catherine and raise a flag there. . . . Then I decided that Andy wouldn't come with us in the boat. For one thing, he wasn't here now, and you could never tell just when this expedition would take place. For another, it would be much more dramatic if Andy arrived in his own plane. He and Ruggles would get out of the plane and would be met by MacDuff and me, with Gunn carrying my sword behind.

Andy would try to take the island and make himself king, because he was a boy. But I would defeat him and MacDuff would rout Ruggles. Then I would graciously allow Andy to marry me and we would be joint rulers of the island. I would have a long blue cloak with a train, which Ruggles would carry behind me. MacDuff would go ahead of me and would be proclaimed Head Dog, with Ruggles far below him in rank . . .

"Sit tight," Mr. Gunn said suddenly. He was staring off to the right. "We're turning back."

I jumped. "Why? I don't want to go back. We can't go back."

"Tak a look at yon fog."

I took a look to his right. The mist was like a white wall that was moving towards us. The coastline of the island was as clear as though it were only six feet off. But I knew it was much farther than that, and when the mist drew level, it would come between us and the coast.

A queer little thrill of fright went through me. Boats were lost in this sea from time to time, usually when people who didn't know better allowed themselves to get caught too far out when the fog suddenly rolled in. Probably that was what Daddy was thinking about when he forbade me to go. But, even though my tummy was fluttering, I wasn't miserable-scared, I was excited-scared.

"Now listen to me," Gunn said, suddenly sounding much less Scottish and more like everybody else. "I should never have let you come along. But you looked that unhappy. . . . If the fog comes between us and the shore, and we don't seem to be getting there as fast as we should, you can trust MacDuff. If anything happens, take his collar, he'll find the shore—as long as it isn't around the point with the tide going out. Do you understand me?"

"Yes. Do you really think we might not beat the fog?"

"It's about fifty-fifty," he said, "but the tide's beginning to turn."

He had swung the boat around and was now rowing towards the shore. I could tell by the way he leaned far forward and pulled at the oars that he was rowing as hard as he could. His hands, brown and rough, looked huge on the oar handles. Dark eyes looked out from beneath the peak of his dirty cap. MacDuff was sitting up, alert. I put my arm around him and watched the fog come towards us like a wall of ghosts come to take us all away. Suddenly MacDuff barked.

"It's all right, lad. We'll make it," Mr. Gunn said, sounding far more friendly than he ever had before.

We did make it. As we pushed the boat up on the shore underneath the jetty, the fog was still out at sea, but it was coming in, fast.

"I've a car on the roadway nearby. I'll tak yer to yer grandmother's."

I sat in the cab of his car, which was a small truck and smelled of fish. MacDuff sat beside me.

"Where do you live, Mr. Gunn?"

"In a wee cottage over on t'other side." I knew we must be safe because Mr. Gunn was sounding Scottish again. Actually, he'd been born in Nova Scotia and had come to Maine when he was a young man. But his parents had been Scottish and he could talk with such a strong accent that nobody understood him. Daddy said he did it deliberately, and Granny said that a language nobody understood was a very useful thing to go into when things got to be too much.

"Can I come and see you and MacDuff?"

"Now, a nice young lassie like yerself would not be wanting to come to a dirty old house."

"Why not? I think I'd like a dirty old house. I wouldn't have to pick up or tidy. And I would have Mac-Duff."

"Aye. He's a good dog. But he's getting on."

"How old is he?"

"I'm not that sure. I found him when he was a young dog. People had left him when they went home after the summer."

"Here on the island?" It didn't sound like anything people on the island would do.

"No. On the mainland, up a piece. He was half starved and savage. He's no so sweet now except with yer. He likes yer. But not many others. Here yer are."

"Good-bye, Mr. Gunn. Good-bye, MacDuff."

"Give her yer paw," Mr. Gunn said.

A large brown paw was held out to me. I shook it. And then I suddenly put my arms around MacDuff's big shoulders and kissed his fur. There was a slight lick in the direction of my ear.

"Yer should feel highly honored, Missie. He doesn't do that often."

"I am." I was thrilled. All the other animals I'd ever known loved everybody else more than they did me. Somehow I didn't mind that MacDuff probably loved Mr. Gunn most of all.

Mr. Gunn spat out the window and drove away, Mac-Duff sitting up on the seat beside him. As they drove up and over the hill, it looked as though they were disappearing into the fog.

The fog wasn't as thick on this part of the bay. I could see the house quite clearly, and the bay water beyond. But everything was gray and fuzzy.

It was funny. I had felt wonderful out on the beach with Mr. Gunn and MacDuff and, even though the fog was coming after us, I had felt wonderful in the boat. Now, facing Granny's house, knowing I had been out long past lunch and that I would have to go in and explain about Elizabeth and the painting and the one hundred and forty-five dollars, I felt terrible. Instead of going in the house, I sat on a boulder at the corner where the path to the house joins the road. Maybe, I thought, the fog would get thicker here, so thick that no one would see me. If I simply went to Gunn's cottage, would he keep me out? Wouldn't he have to let me in so that I wouldn't be lost and die in the fog, because everybody would then blame him? And wouldn't MacDuff stick up for me?

While I was thinking about this, I leaned down and pulled some grass blades from the ground around the rock. Then I put one tight between my thumbs and blew. Usually it makes a kind of moaning sound. But I must have done it righter than I knew. There was a loud, piercing shriek. I heard the sound of a window being raised.

"Cathy? Is that you?"

Then a yellow light shone straight towards me. Granny's fog flashlight, I thought.

"Cathy, I want you to come in here immediately. Do you realize what time it is?"

Maybe around one-thirty, I thought. I glanced at my watch. It was five minutes past three.

"Cathy?"

All of a sudden Granny was standing beside me, her big red slicker on, the moisture standing out all over her face. Reaching out, she took my hand. "Get down. Now come on. Get down."

I thought for a minute, just a minute, about yanking my hand and running away. But then I knew what she'd do. She'd get Steve and Rob, the island's two policemen, away from their lunch and make them go look for me. And I couldn't escape on the ferry because it wouldn't be running in this fog.

"Okay," I said, and got down.

We walked back up the path in silence. When we got inside the side door, Granny took off her slicker and felt my sweater. "You're wet. Go on up and change. That means the sweat shirt and jeans both. Hold up your foot."

I held it up, hanging on to the bannisters of the stairs.

"That's soaked, too. You have loafers upstairs, I know, and fresh socks. Cathy, I want you to change from the skin out and then come down. You and I are then going to have a talk. Have you had lunch?"

"No. But I'm not hungry." And I wasn't. The thought of the talk that Granny and I were about to have made me feel a little sick.

"It doesn't matter whether you're hungry or not.

Alice has fixed some wonderful vegetable soup and you're going to have some. Then we'll talk. I'll expect you down in ten minutes."

When I got to my room, I slouched over to my window and stared out. The fog was moving in strips. At one moment it would be like dirty cotton right on the other side of the glass, at other moments I could see the side of the hill, the Bentons' roof half way around the bay, and the flagpole in their front yard. But I couldn't see the Proudys'. Marianne, who never disobeyed her mother, would probably have had a large delicious lunch, with ice cream to follow, and would now be watching television. Since Granny's favorite way of punishing me was refusing to let me turn on the tube, and if the fog hung on, then that could mean days and days inside the house with no television. Furthermore, with Granny angry, she probably wouldn't let me sleep with her at night. So if I had that horrible dream, with that awful creature chasing me . . .

Her voice called, "Cathy? What's taking you so long?"

Sometime in the past I must have really taken in the way the porch roof slants down right under my window. Because I didn't even think as I pushed the window up and put my foot out on the roof. It was slippery with the wet from the fog, so I'd have to be careful. Suddenly I shivered. It was cold, and Granny was right, I was wet. Quickly I got back in, raced over to the bureau, took out a sweater, a T-shirt and my parka. Then I flew back across the room just as I heard Granny yell, "If you're not down in two minutes, I'm coming up after you."

Sometimes I believe in whatever it is people mean when they talk about fate. Because at that moment the telephone rang. I waited, one foot up on the windowsill, just to see if it was anybody interesting.

Granny answered the extension in the hall. "Hello," she said. And then, "*Andy*, where are you?"

I took my foot off the sill and stood there, almost shivering with excitement. Somehow—and I didn't know how, because Andy could simply be calling from camp for more shirts or something—somehow I knew that everything would now be different.

five

It *was* different, but not the way I had imagined.

By listening carefully to Granny's side of the conversation, I gathered that measles had broken out at Andy's camp, and that he would be here on the island in the late afternoon. He was arriving in Portland by plane and being driven north by car. "Maybe the fog will be gone by then," Granny said.

Andy would be here . . .

I was so excited, I wanted to jump out the window, turn cartwheels, leap up and touch the ceiling. Now I wouldn't be stuck with Marianne. Andy and I would be together the whole summer, and for at least another two weeks before Daddy and Laura came back. We'd do absolutely everything together.

Suddenly it became twice as important that Granny and I not have that conversation. The way she'd sounded when she'd said she wanted to talk to me, she'd probably thought up a whole new set of rules, and I didn't want to know about them. If I didn't know about them, then nobody could expect me to keep them. But the immediate problem was to distract Granny from coming up here and giving me a piece of her mind. And the only way I could think of to prevent her talking to me was to act asleep.

Quickly I stripped off, got into fresh pants and a T-shirt and crawled under my quilt. With my head almost covered, I made slow sounds that weren't quite snoring.

Granny called twice. Then she came up and into the room. I could almost see her take in my wet shirt on the chair, my jeans, sweater and T-shirt on the floor and my socks and pants in the bathtub.

"Cathy?" she said in a much lower voice.

To pretend to ignore her would just make her sure I was faking. It would be better to be half asleep.

"Ummmm," I said, and turned my head on the pillow. It was very artistically done, I thought, which was encouraging, because I had long ago made up my mind that I was going to be an actress when I grew up. I decided to expand the role a bit. "Ummmmm," I said again, drawing it out, sounding even sleepier. I moved my leg and burrowed even more deeply into my pillow. That was exactly the way anyone who really needed a rest would act.

I was therefore not pleased when Granny said, "I am nine-tenths sure that this big sleep you're having is put on, Catherine, to distract me from having the talk with you that I fully intend to have. But, for the sake of that one-tenth doubt, I'm willing to leave you to your nap— if it is a nap, which I don't believe for a minute."

I heard her walk to the door. "You might hang your clothes up when the coast is clear," she said. And then, "It's really too bad you're too sleepy to have lunch. After Alice's vegetable soup, there was peanut-butter-flavored ice cream."

I almost gave it away then. It's my favorite flavor of ice cream, and Granny knows it, and I would have sworn on packs of bibles that she would never have it in the house and was just saying this, hoping to booby-trap me. But I managed—just—not to move.

"Ha!" Granny said. "Very clever. But I saw you nearly leap out of bed. I shall give the rest of the ice cream to Alice's niece, who's visiting in the kitchen." And with that, the door slammed.

It was hard staying up there trying to sleep, which I couldn't seem to do. For one thing, I was so hungry I felt as though my stomach was lying next to my backbone. I kept thinking of the peanut-butter-flavored ice cream. Maybe, just maybe, I thought, Granny really had bought some.

Mind over matter, I sternly told myself. If I was going to be an actress, I would probably have to be on a diet most of the time. As far as I could learn from all the actresses' biographies, that's all they did about food—diet. I turned over and tried to count sheep, but the white woolly bodies going over the fence made me think of Susan, the Siamese, trying to jump onto the rock with her bad leg and missing, all because I had scared her by yelling "Yaaaaahhhhh!" Why had I done that? I wished now, particularly when I thought of Susan falling, that I hadn't done it. For some reason the whole thing made me angry at Elizabeth, the Wicked W., but I didn't know why. And the name Wicked W. didn't apply to her any more anyway. It was silly. It was too fairy-talish, too kiddish, too happy-ending-ish. She was an adult, a real person, a tall woman who painted. The funny thing was, I had two different feelings about her. One was that I liked her a lot. The other was that I was scared of her. . . . But I really didn't want to think about that. Instead, I let my mind drift to the boat, the mysterious, invisible island, Queen Catherine, MacDuff, Head Dog, Gunn, the sword carrier. I went to sleep. . . .

I was running again, and the woman in the long blue robe was after me, the straw hair like yellow snakes coming out of her head. Only now she was much nearer. I could hear her behind me, climbing the rocks, grasping my shoulder, shaking it.

"Hey, wake up! It's me, Andy!"

There, sitting on my bed, was Andy, complete with red hair, blue eyes and a gap between his front teeth.

"Andy!" I said, and sat up.

"Man, you sure were making a noise!"

I reached out my arms to hug him, but he didn't seem to want to be hugged. I drew back. "I guess I must have had a bad dream. Are you here for the summer?"

"Yes. Don and me. And Ruggles. They had measles in the camp. How about that! When you can get a shot against it and everything. People are so stupid."

"I thought the camp people made all the kids have shots for everything."

"Yeah, they're supposed to. Only the kid that got sick, his parents lied. They said afterwards—at least that's what we all heard—that they thought all those shots were just stupid, making doctors and medicine rich. That kind of thing. Anyway, there's talk they're going to be sued. It was a shame. It was a really good place, even if they wouldn't take Ruggles."

Suddenly I took in what he had said. "Is Ruggles here? And who's Don?"

"He's the kid who came home with me. He's going to spend a month here. His folks went away, like ours, so now that camp's closed, he's going to be here. Isn't that super?" Andy got up. "Grandma said to tell you that dinner'll be ready soon. See ya."

I lay there for a minute, trying to fight off a low feeling that had started when Andy'd said he'd brought home Don Whoever-he-was. And Ruggles. But I reminded myself that one of the things about Andy that was so great was that he didn't treat me one way when we were alone and another when he was with his friends.

I got up, slipped into fresh jeans and a clean sweater, put on clean socks and loafers and sat down in front of the little dressing table to brush my hair. Some of the time it feels sort of stupid to do that, as though I were some kind of old-fashioned type who thinks that looks in a female is the only thing that counts. Other times, though, I pretend the dressing table is like the ones in a theatre dressing room that I had seen in an old movie, with lights all around and telegrams stuck in the mirror. I took off the two bands that divided my hair into ponytails, and brushed it. My hair isn't curly, but it isn't quite straight. Brushed straight down, it's shoulder-length. I pulled it back behind my ear on one side and forward on the other. Then I turned sideways and looked at myself in the mirror over my shoulder. One of the things I had bought with some allowance I had saved up was a big book filled with photographs of old-time movie stars from the thirties and forties. Those were the ones who posed looking over one shoulder, with thick eyelashes like fans and hair falling down their bare bosoms. The trouble was, most of those who really looked sultry and mysterious had dark hair. Maybe, I thought, opening the top button of my sweater and pulling it down, and letting my hair fall into what would be my cleavage after I was a little older, I could dye my hair black . . . like . . . like Hedy Lamarr.

"Come weed me to de Caasbah," I said in a throaty voice.

"How about coming weed me to de dining room?" Granny said from the door. "Arise, O glamour queen, your public awaits you."

I pulled up my sweater, pushed my hair back and got

74

up, braced for the talk that I was sure would follow immediately.

"You look all set for the execution chamber," Granny said.

"Well, you said you wanted to talk to me." My words came out sounding as though I was mad, which I wasn't. I was scared.

"Is that why you're holding your breath?"

I let it out. "What was it you wanted to say?" I spoke with as much cool as I could summon.

"I wanted to tell you . . . no, to ask you . . . please never—and Cathy, I mean *never*—just take off again and not show up for meals or when I'm expecting you."

I stared at my toes and didn't say anything. Maybe I could get through without committing myself.

Granny had paused, but when I didn't reply, she went on. "I called Phyllis Proudy, but she said Marianne had gone on to the mainland to see a movie with a friend there. So I knew you weren't with her." More silence. "I then called Elizabeth O'Byrnne, but she said you'd run out of there before your time was finished."

Well, I thought, so Granny knows all about that. I waited for her to forbid me to go back up there. So I was really surprised when she said instead, "Where were you in the interim between running from Elizabeth's house and your turning up here?"

"I took a walk."

"All by yourself?"

"Yes." It was partly true. I did walk to the beach by myself.

"You mean you walked for nearly three hours?"

"I sat on the beach for a while."

"Look, I don't want you to feel as though you were

in a cage. I don't have to know everything you do every minute of the day. I'm a devout believer in privacy and a reasonable amount of freedom. But . . . after what happened to your grandfather . . . and . . . I'm a little nervous about people disappearing on this island and not showing up. It's inclined to activate old wounds and worries."

I hadn't really been sure what she was talking about, but suddenly it made sense. "You mean about Grandfather going out in his boat and never coming back? One of the dragons?"

"Yes, I do mean that. I realize it's unfair to lay some of that burden on you. But that's the way it is. Sometimes, Cathy, we have to make allowances for one another's weaknesses. Do you know what I'm talking about?"

"Not really."

"Hey!" Andy's voice sounded at the foot of the stairs. "The food's all ready and Don and I are starved."

"All right," Granny called down. "I'm sorry. Just possess your soul in patience another minute." She turned back towards me. "Okay, Cathy? Is it a bargain? No more lengthy and unexplained absences?"

"Okay," I muttered. I slid my hand behind my back and crossed my fingers.

We continued to stand there for a minute. "If I had the courage," Granny said, "I'd see if your fingers were crossed behind your back." She was looking straight in my face when she said that. I tried to think cool, but I could feel my cheeks getting warm.

"So they *were* crossed," Granny said. A look that was partly sad and partly something else went over her face. She turned to go downstairs, but said as she went down, "I trust for your sake, Cathy, that you do not decide to take up a life of crime. With a face and complexion like yours, I'm afraid you'd be permanently in jail."

I went downstairs behind her, telling myself that she wasn't that smart, and anyway, how did I know that she'd guess about my fingers.

The first person to greet me when I went into the dining room was Ruggles, who came over, flapping his tail, and sniffed around my hands and legs, probably smelling MacDuff.

"You could at least say hello to him," Andy said.

"Hi, Ruggles," I said without enthusiasm. His tail flapped some more. But after that he went back to Andy and sat right down beside his chair.

"Introduce your friend, Andy," Granny said, sitting down.

Andy's eyes were glued on the big plate of potato salad that Alice had put on the dining table. "Don, that's my stepsister, Cathy. Cathy, this is Don. Can I have some potato salad, Grandma?"

"Don who?" Granny said. "That's only half an introduction."

"Don Ellerby. Can I?"

Granny sighed. "Here you are. Help yourself. Don, you help yourself, too."

I stared at them heaping piles of potato salad onto their plates, trying to fight the low feeling that I'd had upstairs and that was now back, if anything, more strongly. It seemed crazy to think that Andy looked older after only two weeks. But he did. Or something about him was different. Maybe it was being next to Don, who was older. Don was about the best-looking boy I'd ever seen, with dark brown wavy hair, almost gold eyes and a faint brown down on his upper lip and in front of his ears. It almost wasn't there, but that's where I knew he would be getting a mustache and beard. With Andy you couldn't tell that he'd ever grow hair on his face. With Don you knew he would, and soon.

"You're older than Andy aren't you?"

Don didn't answer.

Andy said. "Not much."

"Why can't you answer for yourself?" I asked Don.

He shrugged. "I'll be fourteen in a couple of months."

"Where do you live during the winter, Don?" Granny asked, putting a couple of slices of ham on his plate.

"Westchester."

"Hey, you know that hardware store on the mainland I told you about?" Andy said. "We can go over there after dinner and see if we can get some fishing stuff."

"You can go tomorrow," Granny said. "It may still be light after dinner, but it's too late to try and go to the mainland tonight. Besides, the car's put away."

"We can walk to the ferry, Grandma. It's only seven." Andy said. "And then we'll have the fishing stuff ready for tomorrow morning."

"What's happening tomorrow morning?"

"Pete said he'd take us out in his boat. I saw him when the bus came into the village. I told Don how we could catch fish up here."

I could almost see Granny weaken. Andy isn't even her grandson—the "Grandma" which he likes better than "Granny" is purely honorary. If it was me, I thought angrily, she'd say no. No shopping tonight. Instead, she glanced at the two boys. "Well, I know you keep your promises, Andy. And the beach road is well lit. All right. But remember, you're to be home by nine. No matter what. Promise?"

Andy did a throat-cutting movement around his neck. "I swear or hope to die," he said.

"Please don't. And that applies to you, Cathy, too. Back by nine."

"Sure," I said.

"I thought just Don and me would go to the store, Grandma. It being late," Andy said. He didn't look at me.

"I don't want to go anyway," I said. "I'm going up to see Marianne."

Granny opened her mouth and then closed it. She looked at me. "I want you back by nine, too."

"Okay."

I was back long before nine. Marianne was still furious with me for not showing up at our meeting place on the beach right after twelve.

"I waited an *hour*," she said.

"I'm sorry. I got held up. Doing this extra work in the morning—"

"And your grandmother didn't know a thing about your having bad grades and having to do extra work. You made it up. My mother says—"

"That's all you ever do," I said, "—listen to your mother and say"—I raised my voice—" 'Yes, Mommy,' just like any goody-good girl. It's too bad—"

"And what's more, Mother says you're disturbed. Good-bye."

I watched Marianne's back as she returned up the beach to her house. It was pretty dark now. But the stars were out and Granny was right—the beach road off to the right was well lit.

I knew that Andy, Ruggles and Don were in the

village seeing Pete, who hires out his boat for fishing. Granny was probably reading in the living room and Alice was in her own room watching television.

As I got nearer to the house, my steps seemed to slow down of their own accord. Finally I was in the shadows under the house. Bushes and trees going up the steep bank cut off the road lights. Only the stars and the water and the rocks were left. And the house above with the lighted windows. By this time I was just sliding my feet along, pushing pebbles and sand in front of me. If I went back to the house, I could watch television. Or read a book. Or do both, first television and then read. It was funny. Sometimes I look forward all day to going into my room and reading at night, especially just before I go to bed. But I wasn't now in the middle of a book that I longed to get back to, and—

"Cathy?"

It was Granny's voice. I froze. For a second I wondered if she'd died and was speaking to me as a ghost, the way I saw once in a movie.

"I'm here. Up on the rock."

I looked up towards the top of the big rock formation that is under the house. I hadn't seen her because she was in the darkest part, but now that I had heard her and knew she was there, I could make out her light gray slacks and white sweater.

"There's plenty of room. Want to come up?"

I hesitated, still thinking about that talk she wanted to have with me.

"It's all right. I'm not going to scold you."

"What are you doing up there?" I asked, starting to pick my way over some of the smaller rocks beneath the big one.

"Listening to the water, looking at the stars, smelling the breeze. Want a hand?"

I saw her hand, reached up and took it and she pulled me up beside her onto the big flat top. I wiggled my fanny over so that we were almost back to back. Even though she said she wouldn't scold, I was sort of waiting for her to say something. But she didn't say anything at all. We just sat there. After a while it came to me that if she said she wouldn't scold, she meant it, and she'd keep her word. I guess that was what she was talking about when she said Andy was reliable. I'd always want to be free. But maybe being reliable was a good thing, too. After a while I breathed in and said, "What does the water smell like?"

"Salt, fish, wet, magic."

I sniffed. It was true. It did smell like salt and fish and wet. What did magic mean? I sniffed again. Maybe magic was that extra something in the smell that I'd never smelled anywhere else.

From where we sat we could see around the point to the ocean: gray, with little white lines, making a long, shhhhing noise.

Suddenly I said, "What does 'disturbed' mean?"

"It could mean a lot of things, depending on the context. Upset, bothered . . . what way was it used?"

"Marianne told me her mother said I was disturbed."

"That was nice of Marianne. Used that way, disturbed is just a fancy, fashionable way of saying you don't behave the way she thinks you ought. When I was young, and certainly when my parents were young, Mrs. Proudy would simply have said you were a naughty girl."

"I'd rather she'd say that."

"So would I. But I'm sure she'd tell you that to say you were naughty would be making a value judgment.

And she'd never do anything like that."

"What's a value judgment?"

"It's a piece of sociological jargon meaning judging people."

"What's wrong with that? I do it all the time. I think she stinks."

"Cathy, did I ever tell you how much I like you?"

"No. I don't think so." I wiggled even closer. "You mean you're not mad at me?"

"This little conversation has nothing to do with our current, ongoing disagreement. Right now, it's pax."

"What's pax?"

"It's what we used to say as kids when we were declaring mutual peace. Pax means peace in Latin."

"Oh. Pax, then," I said fervently.

Granny put her arm around me. "And don't let Andy hurt you. He's just now beginning a phase which you're going to find difficult. During this time he would rather be publicly whipped than caught talking to a girl or doing anything different from any of the other young hoods going through the same phase. This phase, you understand, is succeeded by another phase, during which he can't think about anything *except* girls. It's nothing to do with you. It's all nature."

"Nature stinks, too."

"She does, sometimes."

"Why is nature she?"

"Well, I could talk to you about English not having masculine and feminine genders in their pronouns, the way French and Latin do, and that in those languages from which English is partly derived nature is feminine. Or I could say that language, particularly written language, has been developed by men who had a tendency to pronounce as feminine anything that was elemental, powerful and unpredictable—such as a typhoon, a hurricane, the ocean, a large ship or Mother Nature. Or I could simply say it was tradition. Take your pick. There's probably some truth in all of them."

We were silent some more. Then I said, "Do you think about Grandfather when you're out here sitting on a rock?"

"Yes. I think about other things, too. But I do think about your grandfather, and our daughter who was lost with him. I also think about the son who wasn't—your father—and you and Laura."

"Laura's not your daughter," I said, which was so obvious it was silly. "And Andy's not really your grandson, is he?"

"No, and no, to both. But I'm very fond of them."

"Did you know my mother?" As the words came out of my mouth, I wondered where they had come from. I'd never asked them before.

"Yes. I knew your mother."

"What did she look like?"

"Like you. You got your blonde hair and blue eyes from her, along with most of her features. Don't you remember her at all?"

"No. I was only five, or at least that's what Daddy says. I don't really remember. Was she nice?"

Granny didn't answer that right away. Then she said, "She could be. Very. When she was nice . . . well, she was bright and warm and witty. But . . . but when she was ill, she was . . . different."

"Was she ill a lot?"

"She . . . she became, finally, very ill." Granny was saying the words as though she were picking them carefully out of a box, like Scrabble letters.

"Is there something funny I ought to know?" I asked.

"Like what?"

"Like I don't know. But you sound like there is."

"Look, Cathy. Sometime you may suddenly remember your mother. People do remember others from the time they're five, although not always. But you just may. If you do, and you recall her as . . . unpleasant, or even frightening, then remember, she was ill."

"Ill how?"

"It was an illness of the mind as well as the body. And don't judge, Cathy, don't judge."

"That sounds like Mrs. Proudy and not making value judgments."

"I don't mean it quite that way. I mean something that comes out of the heart." I had my mouth open when Granny went on, "And it's no use asking me to explain further, because I can't. Not right now, anyway. And that isn't really what I set out to say to you tonight. What I wanted to say was that for one reason or another you may find this summer difficult. There's really nothing I can do about that. Sometimes when you come to a bad patch, all you can do is walk through, putting one foot in front of another, remembering that it won't last. You *will* get through it. It'll be all right. And I'm here. And I love you."

She put her arm around me, and then I put my arm around her. Usually I have a dozen questions when I don't understand what she's been talking about. But this time I didn't.

"Would you like to share my bed tonight?" Granny asked.

"Yes. Thanks."

six

Neither Granny nor I mentioned my going to sit for Elizabeth O'Byrnne. I guess I thought she wavered between forbidding me to go and not forbidding me to go, and if I mentioned it, she'd waver over to the side of forbidding me.

Granny was alone when I came down to breakfast. "Andy still asleep?" I asked, sliding into my chair.

"No. He and Don went off to catch fish."

I drank some milk and ate half an orange and pushed some cereal around in my dish. "Can I be excused now?" I asked.

Granny, who had been reading the local paper, lowered it and looked at my dish. "You haven't finished your breakfast."

"I'm not hungry."

"Are your clothes picked up and the soiled ones put in the hamper?"

"No. I'll put 'em in now."

"Please," Granny said. Then she smiled. "And thanks. I thank you, Alice thanks you."

Ten minutes later I was downstairs. "Bye," I said, still wondering if she was going to mention my going to Elizabeth's house.

"Cathy, turn around."

I turned. Here it comes, I thought. Maybe she won't like the fact that I'm going to get all that money.

"I want you to be back at one. And if by any chance you decide to stay to lunch at Marianne's or go with her to the mainland, I want you either to come back and tell me, or call me from Mrs. Proudy's house so I can talk to her."

"I thought you didn't like her."

"That's not the point. And what's more, Miss, you know it. Now, do I have your promise?"

This time I didn't cross my fingers behind my back. "Okay. I promise."

"See you at one, then. And if by any chance . . . oh, never mind! Run along."

"If what?"

"Nothing. Have a good morning."

I really didn't want to go to Elizabeth's. I felt bad about yelling and frightening Susan. And she'd want to know why I did it and I wouldn't be able to tell her, and it would end up like one of those grown-up-kid conversations in which the kid always comes out looking bad.

What I wanted to do, I thought, climbing slowly up the hill path to the house, was go out in the boat with Gunn, my sword carrier, and MacDuff, Head Dog. Wouldn't it be terrific if MacDuff had a fight with Ruggles and won, I thought, and wondered if there was any way I could bring this about. When I got to the top of the hill, before I went around it and down to the house, I stopped and stared out to sea. Far out, just a dot in the blue, was a boat. I was pretty sure it was Gunn and MacDuff, fishing. Pete wouldn't take Andy and Don and, probably, Ruggles, out to sea like that. He'd stay in the bay.

After a while the dot got so small I almost couldn't see it, and anyway, the sun was in my eyes, making them water. So I went around the hill and was about to start down the slope to the house, when I decided I'd take a look at my cave.

Actually, it isn't a cave, it's a shelf that juts out about eight feet under the top of the cliff, but you have to be right at the edge of the cliff to see it. Looking around to make sure no one was watching me, I went to the edge and peered over. There it was, a small ledge at the corner of the hill where it turns back to form one side of the cove and the valley where Elizabeth's house is. The funny part is, unless you stand right where I was, you can't see the shelf. At that point, the cliff overhangs the ledge. And there really is a small, shallow cave where the cliff curves back to meet the shelf. It can't be seen from below, either. Once when I was out with Gunn, I had got him to row around just under the point of the cliff. At one particular point, if you knew the shelf was there, you could see it, a shadowy line parallel to the top and just under it, but if you didn't know, it wouldn't look like a shelf, it would just look like a line.

Once, two years before, I'd climbed down to the shelf. It wasn't hard. There were plenty of handholds and footholds. I was hiding from Andy, hoping he'd miss me and get worried. But Ruggles discovered where I was in no time, and stood on top of the point barking until Andy came and looked down. I thought I'd hidden in the cave so that he wouldn't see me. But one of my feet stuck out, so what I heard was Andy's voice saying, "Okay. I see you. That's a pretty stupid place to be. And if you didn't want to be seen you shouldn't have stuck your sneaker out that way."

I hadn't minded going down the edge of the cliff to the ledge at all, but when I wiggled out to see Andy above, I suddenly realized that I was sitting with my fanny half over a shelf with nothing underneath for what looked like a mile, and at the end of the mile rocks and the ocean. Something about that tremendous drop made me just freeze. All I could think of were stories of people who had fallen off or jumped from the cliffs on this, the ocean side, of the island.

"Cathy!" Andy had called. "Don't look down. *Don't look down.* Look at me!" Somehow that had broken the spell. I had looked up. The round, jutting cliff that had been so easy to get down now looked like the Empire State Building.

"It's simple," Andy said. "There're lots of footholds. Do you want me to come down?"

There was something about the rather superior way he'd said it that made me reply, equally casual, "I can manage, thanks." And I did, although I shook for an hour afterwards. I had not been down since.

I stood there at the edge now, thinking about the climb up and down. Then I got down onto my stomach and wiggled until my head was over the edge. The sun on the sea was brilliant, making the water turquoise, almost blinding me. I could see the footholds even more easily, with my nose only about a foot from the top one. Andy was right. It wasn't that hard. But something had happened to me in the two years since I had gone down so lightly. Now I was scared. Just looking over the cliff made my stomach churn and my head feel dizzy. Chicken, I muttered to myself, and then wiggled back, pushing myself with my arms. I didn't feel really at ease until I was ten feet back from the cliff edge.

The house was quiet as I approached, the sun pouring onto the white frame and green shutters. I paused, trying to see through the windows of the big living room, which didn't have any curtains. But I couldn't see anything. When I tried the knob of the front door, it opened, and I walked into the living room to see Elizabeth working on a watercolor at her easel. Because the living room ran the whole width of the house, it had windows on three sides and the light seemed to pour in from everywhere.

"Good morning, Cathy," she said. She had on jeans and a shirt that looked clean because I could see where it had been folded, but it must have had permanent paint stains on it, because there were streaks of green, red and blue across the front.

"Would you like to sit in that window seat over there?"

I went over and sat down. Elizabeth took the sheet she'd been working on from the easel and put it on the piano. Then she put up another sheet and took some charcoal and started to work some more.

I had been sitting there for a while—maybe half an hour—with the feeling that something was wrong, before I suddenly knew what it was.

"Where are Susan and Jason?" I said.

"I put them in my bedroom for the time being. They're just as happy sleeping off their breakfasts on my bed."

I turned to stare out of the window. "You're afraid I'll yell at them again, aren't you?"

"Maybe something about them triggers some antagonism in you."

I could feel the anger growing, starting in my stomach. "Animals are stupid," I said.

90

She didn't say anything.

We sat there for a while not saying anything. She drew. I stared out the window. It was boring. I wished I wasn't there.

"Talk to me about something," she said.

"What do you want me to talk about?"

"Your grandmother tells me that Andy, the stepbrother you're fond of, is here. Isn't he the person you said you most liked to be with?"

"Yes," I said, thinking about Don.

"Are you glad he's here?"

"No."

"Why not?"

I didn't say anything.

"Is it because he's brought a friend?" She wiped one of her brushes on a rag.

I turned my head and shifted my position and then waited for her to tell me to turn back. But she didn't. "Have you been talking to Granny this morning?" I asked.

"As a matter of fact, I have. Why?"

"Because Andy and Don only arrived yesterday evening, so I don't see how she could have told you about them before now."

"Well, we did talk this morning. Anything wrong with that?"

"I don't know. But I think it's funny. First of all, I get the idea that she doesn't want me to come here. Now she talks to you all the time like she arranged the whole thing."

Elizabeth washed her other brushes, one by one, wiping them with a soft cloth.

"Look, Cathy. Let's be friends. Okay? I think what happened with the animals was at least partly my fault.

I shouldn't have dumped them on you when I knew you didn't like them. But—" She turned away and stared out the window. Then I saw her hand reach into her pants pocket and bring out a tissue. She blew her nose. Why, I wondered, was she crying?

"What's the matter?" I said.

She put the tissue away. "I guess I'm having a case of the might-have-beens or I-wish-there-weres."

"Might have been what?"

Elizabeth had turned back to the easel and stared at it in silence. Then, "I'm not at all happy with this. You look stiff. Maybe because I was feeling stiff." She glanced at me. "Why don't you come over and see what you think of it?"

I got off the window seat and went over. I don't know exactly what I'd expected, but I certainly hadn't realized how good she was. There I was in the painting, looking out the window. Outside the window was a land of fantasy. Green stretched almost to the edge of the page, with mountains and a castle in the background. In between were marvelous animals in bright colors.

"It's terrific," I said.

"Do you really like it?" There was a funny note in her voice, as though she was anxious about what I thought—almost afraid I wouldn't like it.

I glanced up at her. Something about her face made me say, "Sure. I think it's great." And then, without think-ign, I took her hand. Her fingers closed over mine. Her eyes looked very bright. After a minute she took her hand away and turned back to the painting. "I'm glad you like it, but I'm still not entirely satisfied with your figure in the painting. Look at it again and tell me what you think—honestly."

I peered at the picture of myself. There were my ponytails and profile. But it was true. The drawing of me was not as vivid or full of life as the animals. I stared at it.

"Maybe," I said, "if it was really me, I'd be trying to get out of the window. I wouldn't just be sitting there with my hands in my lap."

"I think you're right."

She picked up a piece of charcoal and made some strokes with it. Suddenly the girl in the picture came to life, her hand reaching up to unfasten the window.

"Yes, yes," I said excitedly. "That's right. That's much better."

Elizabeth took up an eraser and wiped off the old drawing. She hadn't painted that part of the paper yet, so it was easy to draw in the new pose. Then she put some finishing touches on the new drawing. "You have a good eye, Cathy. Have you ever drawn?"

"Yes. One term, years ago. But I didn't like the teacher, Miss Diggs."

"Was that the only reason?"

"Well, she always said I didn't know how to draw. Then she'd rub out whatever I'd done and draw her own thing on top of it. She made me mad."

"I can see where she would. Would you like to try some pictures of your own?"

The moment she said it, I knew I would. But then there was the bicycle that I wanted. "What about posing for you?"

She looked at me for a minute. "Are you worried about the money?"

I thought she might act funny if I said yes. Grown-ups sometimes do. I looked down and muttered, "Well, I *said* I was going to pose for you."

"Look at me," she said.

I looked up.

"I can draw you while you're drawing pictures. If I want you to strike a particular pose for a minute, I can always ask. But you'll have the money anyway. After all, I did . . . I did commission your time each day. Here." Quickly she went over to where canvases were stacked and pulled out another easel, smaller and lighter than the one she was using. She set it up. "This is the one I used to use. Here's some paper and a piece of charcoal. Why don't you have a try? In the meantime, I'll be finishing off this and blocking in another."

I took the charcoal between my fingers and thumb and stood staring at the paper.

She held out her hand holding the charcoal. "Hold it like this. It'll feel strange at first, but you'll have more freedom. See?"

I looked at the way she was holding her piece and copied it.

"Okay," she said. "Now draw something."

I stood in front of the paper not knowing what to draw. "What shall I draw?" I asked.

"Anything you like. You can draw me, or that tree out there, or the edge of the cliff, or the piano or pictures to go with a story you make up."

After a minute and without planning, I started to draw Susan, the cat, with a head with ears on top and whiskers going out each side, a body and a tail: one circle on top of another circle. But that wasn't really Susan. That was any cartoon cat.

"Can I borrow your eraser?" I asked.

Elizabeth tore her eraser in half and gave me one part. "Here." She came over and looked at my drawing as I was rubbing it out. "You ought to go and look at Susan and then draw her from life—just as you see her."

"All right." I put down the piece of charcoal. "Can I go into your bedroom?"

"Of course. Come along, I'll go with you."

The bedroom was on the other side of the little hall. When Elizabeth and I went in, Jason and Susan were curled up on the bed, looking almost like a black and white fur cover. Jason raised his head and his tail began to thump. But when I walked over, Susan jumped off the bed and went under it. I just stood there, feeling terrible. "It's because I yelled at her," I said. "I didn't mean to scare her. Now she hates me."

Elizabeth put her hand on my shoulder. "Not hate. She is frightened at the moment, but if you're gentle around her, she'll get over it."

"That's why I don't like animals. They make me feel terrible." And I turned and went out of the room. I was staring at a new blank piece of paper when I heard Elizabeth come across the floor. She passed me and went to the window seat on the other side of the easel. In her arms she was carrying Susan. "Now," she said when she sat down. "I'm going to hold her and stroke her gently, and in a minute I want you to come over quietly and stand here, so she'll get used to you. Then maybe she'll let you touch her and she'll see you don't mean to frighten her."

I opened my mouth to say I didn't care whether Susan liked me or not. But at that moment she started to purr as Elizabeth rubbed her head between her ears and stroked her back. Slowly Susan's crossed blue eyes closed. Slowly her purr got louder.

"Now," Elizabeth said in a quiet voice, "why don't you try to draw her?"

By this time Susan was curled in a circle in Elizabeth's lap.

I drew a round line in the middle of the page.

"Don't make it too small," Elizabeth said suddenly, but still very quietly. "Take up the whole page."

I rubbed out the line I'd done and drew a big circle. Then I put a triangular head and two ears on the bottom of the circle, and was amazed at how much it looked like Susan curled up.

I stepped back and glanced at Elizabeth. She smiled and I smiled back. Then I went over and stood in front of Susan. In a minute Elizabeth, who was still rubbing Susan between her ears, lifted her hand and I continued rubbing her on the same spot with the same rhythm. Susan opened her eyes immediately. I could feel her tense.

"Good Susan," I said quietly.

She was staring at me, eyes wide open. Then the lids came slowly down and she relaxed. I went on rubbing, then started stroking her back. But when I stooped to pick her up, Elizabeth said quickly, "I wouldn't. Not just now. Give her a chance to come to you first."

I stepped back and went over to the easel, where I started filling in the drawing.

"I didn't mean to frighten her," I said. "I don't know why I yelled like that."

"We all do things we don't mean to do. And the awful part is we do it to the people we want most to like us."

I looked at her. "Have you done it? Frightened some-body you liked a lot?"

"Oh yes."

"Who?" I said, and then wondered if she'd think I was nervy.

Elizabeth leaned back against the window. She wasn't

stroking Susan any more. Susan seemed sound asleep.

"My daughter."

"I didn't know you had a daughter. You didn't mention her when I asked you before."

Elizabeth didn't say anything.

"You scared her? Your daughter, I mean?"

"Yes."

"How?"

"Yelling at her. Threatening her. Scolding her."

"And now you're sorry?"

She smiled a little. "Very sorry indeed."

I finished the drawing and stepped back, looking at it. It was really very good, I decided, and a great, warm happiness rushed through me.

"Look," I said. Taking the sheet off the easel, I held it so she could see it.

"Cathy, that's really good. You have talent."

I put it back on the easel again and stood looking at it.

"Roll it up and put an elastic band around it. You can take it home that way and tape it to your wall where you can see it all the time."

"All right. Where'll I find rubber bands?"

"In the first drawer of that little cabinet over there. I'd get up but my lap is full."

"It doesn't matter. I can get it."

I ran over and opened the drawer, saw the box of rubber bands, brought one back to the easel and rolled up my drawing. "Can I have another sheet of paper?"

"Take all you want. Just tear them out of that big sketch pad there."

"What'll I draw this time?"

"Why don't you make up a story and draw illustrations for it as you go along?"

Suddenly I found myself thinking about Gunn, his boat, MacDuff, Head Dog, the imaginary island, Queen Catherine, Ruggles, who would be Slave Dog, and Andy, whom I suddenly demoted from King-consort to prisoner of war. . . .

"Do you know a story?" Elizabeth asked.

"Yes."

"All right. Lead on MacDuff."

I almost jumped. "Why did you say that?"

"It's just an expression." She was looking at me. "It comes from *Macbeth*, Shakespeare's play." She hesitated. "Why?"

I shrugged. "It's just that I know somebody named MacDuff."

"Oh, who? Somebody new on the island? I don't remember any MacDuffs from previous years."

"Just a friend," I said carelessly.

Sometime later I heard Elizabeth say, "Is there anywhere you should be right now?"

I came to with a start. The rolled-up drawing of Susan lay on the floor beside the easel. Propped up on the easel was a second one of Gunn, MacDuff and me in a boat. Gunn was in the front of the boat, rowing. MacDuff was sitting on the seat in the middle of the boat, his paw holding an upright shield. My shield. I was sitting in the back of the boat. There was a round gold band on my head. The name of the boat was painted on the side: *The Queen Catherine*. Far off was the imaginary island with huge fir trees coming down to the water's edge. Even I could tell the drawing was pretty good, though it didn't, of course, look exactly the way I wanted it to. MacDuff's paw, for instance—there was something wrong with it. I was trying to figure out what it was when I heard Elizabeth come up behind me.

"Cathy, it is truly good. I'm not just saying it to cheer you on. You have talent and you should develop it."

I felt really wonderful, and it was because of something I'd done, which I couldn't remember ever happening before. "There's something not right about MacDuff's paw," I said.

"Is that the friend you were talking about? MacDuff?"

I giggled a little. "Yes."

Elizabeth smiled. "So you don't really hate animals."

"I don't like them when they don't like me. And I don't like them when somebody I like says they like an animal better than they like me."

"I see. That's very understandable." Her voice sounded funny. "Do you have anybody in mind?" she asked.

"Not especially," I said as airily as I could, knowing I was thinking about Andy. I heard her breathe in. "Have you got a cough or something?"

"More something than a cough. Cathy—"

But my mind was back on the painting. "Look, what's wrong with MacDuff's paw? And Gunn's hands look funny, too."

There was one of those odd silences. Then Elizabeth said. "Where's your piece of charcoal?"

I handed it to her.

"Dogs have a kind of knuckle here, near the paw itself. So if he was sitting with his paw on the shield, it would bend here a little. And then there's his thumb, which is further up his leg."

Quickly she rubbed out the paw I had drawn and

sketched in her own. It made a lot of difference. "And Gunn's hands are too big for his size, and they'd be turned a little. Like so."

At that moment the phone rang. Elizabeth handed me the charcoal and went over to the telephone. "Hello," she said. And then, "Yes, she's here. I'll put her on. I'm sorry. It's partly my fault. We were both at work and I didn't think about the time until a minute ago. Cathy?" She held out the phone to me.

It was Granny. "You promised, Cathy, to telephone me if you were not coming home to lunch. It's now after one."

"I'm sorry, Granny. I didn't mean to forget. Truly. But I've been drawing a picture. Elizabeth says I'm really good. Don't you?" I appealed across the room.

"You are. Very good." Elizabeth spoke with a smile and in a loud voice. "I hope your grandmother can hear me."

"I heard that," Granny said. "Congratulations! If you hadn't been so mad at Miss Diggs, you might have discovered it sooner. But what about that promise?"

"I really forgot the time, Granny. Honestly."

I heard her sigh. "All right. But I want you to leave this minute and come home to lunch."

"I'm not hungry, and Elizabeth is showing me where I went wrong. Please, Granny—"

"No," Granny said. "Let me speak to Elizabeth."

"She wants to talk to you," I said, holding out the telephone. "She doesn't sound really mad, but she wants me to come home."

Elizabeth took the phone. "It's Elizabeth," she said into the receiver. Then she listened for a while. "All right. I'll send her home." And she put down the receiver.

"Cathy, I'm going to send you home right now. Your grandmother is waiting lunch for you."

"But I'm not hungry and I want to finish this."

Once more she put her hands on my shoulders. "I wish you could. But I promised your grandmother and I have to keep it."

"Why?" I asked sulkily.

"Because she has been very good to me. Because I know she's right. Because she has your welfare at heart. Because . . . well, Cathy, just because. Listen to her and be nice to her. I'll see you tomorrow morning. We'll work on your drawing first thing. I promise."

She was standing at the window as I left. When I got to the curve in the road where it goes around the hill, I turned around. She was still there. I waved and she waved back.

seven

It was funny, but after that everything changed. Instead of the two hours at Elizabeth's being something I had to get through for the money so that I could enjoy the rest of the day with Marianne, it started being the most important part of the day, not because I was posing, or even for the one hundred and forty-five dollars, but because I was doing my own book—a story about Gunn and MacDuff and me and Andy and Ruggles and the magic island—and doing the drawings for it. Of course, the drawings weren't as good as Elizabeth's, and I'd only just begun to learn how to use the watercolors and they ran sometimes, so that in one painting, until Elizabeth helped me wash it out, the boat was yellow instead of my hair, but they looked like real drawings. I never stayed past a quarter to one, not because I was itching to get out of there, the way I used to, but because Elizabeth would say, "Time to go home for lunch now, Cathy." And I'd have to go.

Once I said, "Can I come back?"

She didn't answer right away, but then she said, "No, I'm afraid not. I have to do . . . other things in the afternoon. I'm sorry." She looked up at me. "I really am. I wish . . . well, I wish a lot of things. But you have to go back to your grandmother's now. I'll see you tomorrow, okay?"

I stopped minding so much that I almost never saw Andy, who was always out doing something with Don. I did mind, at least at first, that Marianne seemed permanently angry that now I was never free to play until after lunch. And the fact that I wouldn't tell her what I was doing in the mornings didn't help.

"I know you're not studying the way you pretended," she said a few days later, after trying for the fifth time to find out.

Finally, I said, "It's a secret. I'll tell you after . . . after it's over." When I said that, I felt strange and unhappy, as though I knew it would be over.

"What's over?"

"The secret."

"I thought we were best friends. Best friends don't keep secrets."

"You're only my island best friend. Janet Murray is my all-year-round best friend."

"Are you going to tell her?"

"I don't know!" I shouted. "Why can't we just hang around the way we used to? Why do you have to know everything?" And then I stamped off.

The day after that, I went with Granny to the mainland for the afternoon. She asked me if I wanted to invite Marianne and I said no. The following day when I went to collect Marianne around two in the afternoon, I discovered she wasn't there.

"Marianne's on the mainland today," Mrs. Proudy said in her flutey voice. "She has a friend there now and has gone to play with her. Anne Low. Do you know her?"

"No," I said, although I did.

"She's the daughter of Judge Low. Such a pleasant girl. It's so nice for Marianne to have a friend she can rely on—somebody who doesn't make up stories about what she's supposed to be doing in the morning."

I stared back into Mrs. Proudy's squinty little eyes.

"I forgot. I do know Anne Low," I said. "Granny knows her, too. She says she's the stupidest girl in the entire summer colony." And I turned and walked off before Mrs. Proudy had a chance to say something.

As soon as I stopped being mad, I started being sorry. Mrs. Proudy would almost certainly telephone Granny and tell her what I had said. And while Granny *had* said that Anne Low was not the brightest girl on the northeast seaboard, she might not be pleased at the way I had put it more strongly to Mrs. Proudy.

I was so sure that Mrs. Proudy would make straight for the telephone the moment I left, that I decided not to go back to the house, but to go to the beach to find Gunn and MacDuff.

I came on them just as Gunn was about to push the boat into the water and I climbed in beside MacDuff, who was on the middle seat.

"I told yer," Gunn said. "Yer not comin' out in the boat with us." His breath smelled funny, funny in an unpleasant way that made me uncomfortable.

"Piew!" I said, hoping to distract him. "What have you been eating?"

He grinned and started pushing the boat into the water. "Not eating," he said, and then, as the boat shot into the ocean, he climbed in, his boots dripping. "Drinking."

"Drinking what?"

"Whiskey."

"That's bad for you."

"Yer a fine one to say that!"

"What do you mean? I don't drink. Daddy and Laura practically never drink at all—just sometimes when they

104

have people to dinner, but not at ordinary times."

But Gunn just went on grinning. "Yer wait till yer grow up."

"Pooh! I'm not going to drink when I grow up. It makes people act terrible."

"And how do yer know that, little Miss?" Gunn had a sly look on his face.

"Daddy says so. I've heard him."

"Oh, he does, does he! Well, he ought to know."

"Why?"

Silence. Gunn pulled at the oars and stared at the shoreline we were leaving.

"Why?" I asked again.

"Now stop bothering me with a lot of questions."

"Well, you shouldn't say something and then—"

"Because if yer don't, then I'll turn the boat around and take yer back quick like a flash. And there'll be no more comin' out in the boat with me."

I opened my mouth. I like to have the last word in a fight. But I knew that Gunn would do just what he said—take me back. And if he took me back, what would I do then? Andy was with Don, and Marianne was on the mainland with Anne Low. . . .

I closed my mouth and stared out over the water. Then I put my arm around MacDuff, who lay down and put his big head on my lap again.

"MacDuff," I said, stroking his head, "I like you."

He looked up at me out of his gold eyes, his eyebrows wrinkled. I bent down and kissed him between his ears. He licked my face.

*   *   *

After a while Gunn stopped rowing and picked up a couple of fishing rods from the bottom of the boat. He handed me one. "Fish!" he said.

I'd never fished before, but it didn't seem complicated, so I took the pole from him.

"Here, yer can use this for bait." Gunn handed me a squirmy piece of pinkish meat.

"Yuch!" I said.

"This is no time for fancy feelings," Gunn said. "Put it on the hook."

I put the bait on the hook and flung the line over the boat. Then I sat.

The sun was hot. There was the magic smell that Granny talked about coming over the water; the boat rocked gently. MacDuff went to sleep and started to snore. So did Gunn. When I heard the sound coming from him, I looked over. I couldn't think how he'd keep his line over the boat if he was asleep, but then I saw that he had wedged it down a metal ring and behind a block at the bottom of the boat.

My mind drifted onto my story. . . . Andy was a prisoner of war, with guards outside his wing of the palace. Each day he would send Ruggles with a written proposal of marriage in his mouth to the throne room where I sat, ruling the island, with Gunn holding my sword on one side, and MacDuff holding my shield on the other. Ruggles would be allowed into the throne room, but not only would he have to bow to me, he'd have to bow to Mac-Duff as well. After he'd done that with sufficient humility, he would be allowed to give Andy's note to MacDuff, who would bring it to me and put it on my lap. Then I would have to decide whether 1) I would accept the proposal, 2) I would share my kingdom with Andy or 3) demand ransom from his kingdom beneath the big cave at the bottom of the sea. . . .

"There's a fish on yer line," Gunn said.

"Oh!" I jumped a little and then saw—and felt—that there was something on my line. I pulled the rod up.

"Gently, gently, little Miss! Yer don't want to frighten it now. Don't jerk yer line like that. Reel it in slowly!"

I turned the wheel at the base of the rod as steadily as I could. "What do you think it is?" I asked.

"We'll see, if you don't scare it away."

MacDuff was now standing on the seat, his nose over the side of the boat, watching. I kept turning the wheel and eventually saw a big silver shape flipping and flapping in the water. I reeled and it struggled and flip-flopped. Gunn leaned away over and held the rod steady. Eventually the fish was up in the air.

"Now bring it over to the boat," Gunn said.

I swung it over and lowered the rod so that the fish was in the bottom of the boat, flopping around.

"Now take it off the hook," Gunn said.

The poor fish was bleeding around the mouth, but I got the hook out.

"Watch out, or it'll flap in the water again," Gunn yelled.

I could almost feel its lungs gasping for water.

"Now put yer hand in its mouth and crack its neck. It'll be dead then," Gunn said.

I picked it up and threw it into the water where it could breathe and live.

There was a long silence.

"Ye'll no make a fisherman at that rate," Gunn said. "Yer daft!"

"I didn't want to kill it."

Gunn took the rod away from me, reeled in the line and put it at the bottom of the boat. "And do yer have fish in yer granny's house now?"

"Yes." I knew what was coming next.

"And just how do yer think the fish yer eat was caught?"

"Maybe I should be a vegetarian."

"Aye, maybe yer should."

I sat there while Gunn fished and MacDuff went back to sleep. After a while I grew sleepy. There was a coiled rope in the back of the boat, with MacDuff's shawl over it. Slipping off the seat, I lay down on the rope and stared up at the blue sky. After a minute MacDuff came and curled up with me. I started planning the drawings I would do the next morning. There would be Ruggles with Andy's letter in his mouth, his head and front paws down in front of MacDuff. Perhaps I should put a small coronet on MacDuff's head, just between his ears. . . . Andy would have on a tunic and long hose, like the page in one of Granny's history books. And, of course, he would have chains around his legs. He would be very sad, not only because he was a prisoner of war and I had refused his three proposals of marriage, but because he would have just discovered that his friend, Don, had betrayed him. . . .

"Wake up. It's time yer went home and had some fish for dinner."

I sat up. Gunn was pushing the boat up on the sand. MacDuff woke up, too, shook himself and jumped out. I followed him.

"Are you mad at me for throwing the fish back?" I asked Gunn.

He grinned. "No. Yer've got a soft heart. It's not a bad thing—in a gurl."

The nearer I got to home, the slower I walked, because I knew that the moment Granny said, "What have you been doing this afternoon?" I would be in trouble. I couldn't believe that Mrs. Proudy hadn't been on the phone, and going out with Gunn in his boat had been forbidden by Daddy. As I moved slowly along the beach, kicking the sand and pebbles as I went, I tried the sound of various answers to the question Granny was certain to ask: I was in the village. Doing what, I wondered? The village is tiny, and I could not have spent the whole time since lunch having milk shakes in the drugstore. The only other store is the all-purpose grocery and dry goods, which also carries paperback books, but the only people who spend hours there are middle-aged women who, Granny says, use it as a kind of meeting place. So that left the village out. I could say I'd been going back and forth on the ferry, but if Granny had been on the mainland, then she'd know in a minute I was lying. I could, maybe, have been visiting somebody on the mainland, but who? Anne Low was the only kid my age who was there this summer. . . .

I was still wondering what I'd say when I tiptoed past the living room on my way up to my bedroom. If I could manage not to see Granny until dinner, when Andy and Don would be there, then she might not be so determined to find out where I'd been.

I'd just put my foot on the bottom step when I heard Granny's voice. "Cathy? If that's you, I want to

109

have a word with you. I'm in the living room."

Maybe, I thought, she'd think it was Andy, so I went up on the next step. But it didn't work.

"Yes, I thought it was you. Come into the living room."

Her voice was right behind me. I turned. She had a funny, quirky smile around her mouth. She waited until I came back down and walked over to her, then she put her arm around my shoulder. "Now if you had just not tiptoed, I might have thought it was Andy. I say might, but I think I would know your step, so all your attempts at concealment came to naught."

We went into the living room, which occupies the back quarter of the house and has windows all along two sides. Immediately outside the window a grassy bank slants down. Below that is a strip of bushes, then the beach and then the ocean. The sun, which was low, turned the middle of the ocean into a sort of reddish purple. On either side, the water was gray with white caps.

Without thinking, we went over to the windows and stared out. "Cathy," Granny said, just as I knew she would, "where were you this afternoon? I know you went over to Marianne's house because Mrs. Proudy called me." I waited, braced, for her to repeat to me what Mrs. Proudy had said about what I'd said. But Granny just stood there, her hands in the pockets of her tweed skirt.

Frantically I tried to think up a lie I could get away with. But none came, which for me was unusual. Normally I have no trouble in that direction.

"Well?" Granny said. But she didn't sound angry.

I took a breath. The words, *I was out in Gunn's boat*, had taken shape in my mouth and I was about to say them aloud, when Andy's voice said, "You were out

110

in Gunn's boat. Don and I saw you. How'd you like fishing?"

I turned quickly. Andy and Don were standing in the doorway, with Ruggles panting on the floor at their feet. They must have been running, I thought, and arrived just in time to keep me from ever knowing for sure how I would have answered Granny. I looked at Andy. "Fink!" I said.

"What d'ya mean? Why am I a fink? What's gotten into you?"

"Because you know how Daddy feels about me going out with Gunn."

"How should I know that? He didn't tell me not to. I guess it's because you're a girl," he said.

"Then why did you mention it?"

"Because Pete can't take us out tomorrow. He's already booked to take somebody else out. I thought I'd ask Gunn, but every time I've asked him before, he always spits and says no, he doesn't take people out. So how come he takes you out?"

"Maybe he likes Cathy's company," Granny said. "You and Don go up and wash your hands and put on clean shirts before dinner."

"Do we have to? We put on clean shirts—"

"Yes," Granny said. "And you, too, Cathy. But wait a minute, because there's something we have to talk about."

"I can go up now and—"

Granny put her hand on my shoulder. "In a minute. Off you go, boys."

When they'd gone she said, "I wish they hadn't burst in with their information just when they did. I was pretty sure you were out with Gunn, too, but I was waiting to see whether you would have told me. Do you know what you would have said?"

I looked up into her dark brown eyes. "I think I was going to tell you. But I don't know."

There was a short silence, then Granny said, "As I told you, I talked to Mrs. Proudy this afternoon. I wish, Cathy, that if you're going to quote me, you'd at least do it accurately. I didn't say Anne Low was the stupidest girl in the summer community. I just said—or implied—she wasn't the brightest."

I didn't say anything.

"Look," Granny said, and sat down on the window seat, facing me. "What's the name of that girl you like so much in New York? Janet something?"

"Janet Murray," I said. "Why?"

"Where is she right now?"

"Out at her family's summer house in the Hamptons, I guess."

"How about calling her and letting me speak to her mother. I'll invite her here for the next week. Your father and Laura will be back after that and a couple of the families who come up here regularly will be here and may have some children your age. I'm well aware that your father considers Gunn an unreliable escort, particularly when out in the middle of the ocean. But I also know that it's not easy for you and it wouldn't be fair to you, or the boys, if I forced Andy and Don to take you along. I don't think you'd like it, would you?"

I was still staring down. There was a long dirt stain on my jeans and I was nervously brushing at it with my fingernail. "No," I said, "I wouldn't like it. I wish—"

"You wish what?"

"Nothing."

"Well, I wish you had somebody friendly to play with. The people who're already up here have children of the wrong age. Andy has his own friend, and Marianne is in a snit because you won't tell her where you go in the mornings. Just as a matter of curiosity, why don't you tell her? After all, it was Marianne who first teased you into going to see the Wicked Witch."

Since it was just a feeling—even if it was a strong feeling—it was hard to explain. I didn't say anything.

"Do you just sit and pose up there at Elizabeth's? I should think that by this time she'd have been able to do four books."

"No." I paused. I really hated talking about it. But I found I hated it less with Granny than with anyone else. "Sometimes I draw, too."

"Yes. I know. What do you draw?"

"Oh . . . anything. Her cat, Susan. A story."

"Why don't you bring one of your drawings home so I can see it?"

I thought about my drawing of Susan still in my drawer upstairs. Each night I'd pull it out, take off the band, unroll it and look at it. But then I'd put it away again. I was afraid that if I put it on my wall and somebody came in, then I'd have to answer a lot of questions. In some strange kind of way I felt that as long as my drawing, like my posing for Elizabeth, was a secret, then I could keep it. But if I told anybody besides Granny about it, or showed my drawing, then I might lose it all.

"If you don't want me to see your drawing, you don't have to show it to me. Sometimes it's important to keep something like that a secret."

I looked up. "Yes. It's like that."

She smiled. I burst out, "But if I show it to anybody, I'll show it to you."

"Thank you. That's nice. Now, would you like to telephone Janet to see if she can come and spend some time with you?"

"I'd love to. Can I do it now?"

"The phone is all yours. But when you get her and she says she wants to come here, let me talk to her mother. All right?"

"Okay." I went out to the hall where the telephone sat. It took a little while to get her on the phone. I didn't remember her Long Island phone number, so I had to ask Information and that took time, but finally somebody picked up the receiver and I asked for Janet. "It's long distance," I said, feeling important.

But when Janet came to the phone, it was to tell me that she really couldn't leave now. "It's not that I wouldn't adore to come up there, Cathy, it's just that I'm supposed to crew for my brother in the boat race. And it's the first year he's let me do *anything*. He's always said I was more of a pest than a help, but now he says I'm just the right ballast or something, and I'm going to help in the race. The doctor says it's okay if I don't do anything too strenuous. Could I came up after that?"

But by then Daddy and Laura would be here and it would be different. "I'll call you again when Daddy and Laura get here," I said, trying not to sound as though I wanted to cry, which I did. And I didn't know whether I was crying because Janet couldn't come or because her brother was going to let her crew for him. I could see Andy letting me do anything like that!

114

I was still sitting beside the telephone when Granny came out of the living room. "Well?"

"She can't come. Her brother's going to let her crew for him in a race." It was funny. Granny had only produced the idea a few minutes before, but I felt as let down as though I'd been thinking about it for days.

Granny said, "Never mind. I'll try and patch up your peace with Mrs. Proudy and say something to put off Marianne's burning desire to find out what you're doing."

I looked at Granny and knew that she knew how I felt, which was really astounding. I never thought that anyone ever knew how I felt. I'd lied to practically everybody, including Granny, and been rude to Mrs. Proudy and not been really nice to Marianne and disobeyed lots of unimportant things, like not taking my sweater when I'd been told to. If it were Daddy I was doing these things to, he'd be furious. Even Laura would be impatient, although she gives in a lot because I'm not really her daughter. Granny didn't give in. I didn't have any of what Daddy calls Actual Evidence to go on, but I had a tremendously strong feeling that if I did anything really wrong, Granny'd let me know it in a minute. But she knew how I felt without being sappy or sentimental in a silly way that would make me uncomfortable.

"Thanks," I said. "That'd be really nice. But I don't think you're going to stop Marianne from trying to find out about my posing."

"I suppose not. But I could say that you're engaged in a special project in the mornings."

"Yes," I said. "And then I could tell her that I

couldn't really talk about it because it was *your* secret, couldn't I?"

Granny sighed. "You know, Cathy, I don't like lies. Not even white lies." I had been looking at Granny. But now I stared down at my sneakers. "Yes," she said. "I know you tell them sometimes. Given . . . given the circumstances, I suppose I understand . . . but I still don't like them. Do you know why?"

I shrugged. "I guess because they're wrong."

"Do you know why they're wrong?"

"Not really."

"Because they put a permanent distortion in things as they are and those distortions have effects. I once told an old friend that a dress she'd bought looked attractive, although I knew it looked hideous. When she asked me what I thought about it, I didn't have to tell her that it looked terrible. I could have said something like it didn't suit her as well as some other dress, or the color wasn't her best color. Anything that was reasonably near the truth. But to save her feelings I told a total lie. So she went on wearing that wretched dress and bought another just like it, cheerfully thinking she looked marvelous. I would have done her a much greater service if I'd told her a diplomatic version of the truth. You don't have to be cruel, but you do have to put yourself on the line when you tell the truth, and take the results. In the long run it's better. Do you see what I mean, Cathy?"

"I suppose so. So what do you want me to tell Marianne?"

"Maybe just tell her that it's none of her business."

"She won't like it."

"No, she won't. But if Mrs. Proudy makes any noises about it, I'll back you up—that it's none of her business."

116

I stared back at Granny. It had suddenly occurred to me that it was strange Granny didn't tell me to go ahead and say what I was doing in the mornings. But my mind was still on the business of truth-telling. "Do you *never* tell lies?"

"As seldom as I can manage." She turned. "All right, boys, there has to be a slightly less noisy way to come downstairs."

Andy and Don were coming down, leaping two and three steps at a time and sounding like a falling sack of bricks.

"You mean you never tell lies, Grandma?" Andy said, catching the last of the conversation, the way he often did.

"As I have just said, as rarely as I can manage. For one thing, when I tell one lie, I frequently have to back it up with six others, and, aside from any moral viewpoint, it's a nuisance. Did you boys wash your hands?"

Both said yes.

"Cathy? Have you washed yours?"

"No, Granny."

"All right. You can wash in that little bathroom under the stairs. But hurry. Dinner's ready."

The next day I finished painting the six illustrations I had done for my book while Elizabeth drew me.

"All right," she said, when I told her I was done. "You can type the story on that typewriter over there, and then we can insert the paintings and sew the whole thing together. Do you know how to type?"

"No."

"It's a good skill to have, no matter what you decide

to do with your life. When you get to high school and you have a chance, take it. Your story isn't that long. Why don't you print it carefully, and then, if necessary, I'll type it for you."

"Would you really?"

"Of course. I type all my own books. But see how carefully you can print it, because, if it's done nicely, it'll look even better that way."

I took the drawings off the easel and put them on the table. "Do you really think they're good?"

"What do you think?" she asked. As I looked at her, a little surprised, she said, "It's very important to be honest with yourself about what you think about your own work. Modesty and conceit shouldn't have anything to do with somebody who creates something. What you think of your own work is important. Here, put them like this so you can see them properly." And Elizabeth slid the two easels together, and placed the drawings, which were on smaller pieces of paper than the one I'd done of Susan, one right after the other.

I stood and looked at them for a while, and I found I felt opposite things all at once. I was terrifically pleased and I thought they were really very good. I was also disappointed they weren't better. The island, the boat, a distant castle and MacDuff and Ruggles were good. The scenery was even better. In all the pictures the trees were wonderful—all different greens with pink cherry blossoms and yellow forsythia, the way they are in the spring in Central Park. The people weren't as good. "The people aren't good," I said. "But the dogs and the boat and the scenery are."

"Yes, I agree with you. They're excellent. Drawing

people isn't easy. But you can take classes for that. And you do have an ability to make your people look as though they'd been caught in action. Most amateurs have human figures that are static. I think you have a lot of natural ability and you should take drawing classes when you go back to school. Just straight, classic drawing. Not what I call creative smearing."

I don't know what Granny said to Mrs. Proudy, or even to Marianne, but the next day after lunch, when I was wondering whether to go and find Gunn, Marianne came up on our porch and rang the bell.

"I wonder who that is," Granny said. She was drinking the last of her coffee.

I looked out the window. "Marianne." I was surprised.

Granny got up. "Bearing an olive branch, no doubt."

"Doing what?"

"An olive branch is a peace symbol."

"Oh. I guess Anne Low was busy this afternoon."

"Now you listen to me, Miss Feist. Be nice. If she asks you to go pick fleas off a monkey, you tell her that's what you most wanted to do this afternoon."

I giggled. By that time, Alice had answered the door and Marianne was in the dining room.

"Hi," she said.

"Hi," I said. I could feel Granny's eyes on me all the way across the dining room.

"I was wondering if you wanted to go over on the ferry and have a milk shake at the drugstore."

"Sure. That'd be nice."

We were about to say good-bye to Granny when something very strange happened. Andy and Don came downstairs on their way out.

They stared at Marianne and she stared back.

"Don, this is Marianne Proudy," Granny said. "Marianne, you know Andy, Cathy's brother, and this is his friend, Don."

All four of us just stood there. Granny, who had been gathering up the lunch plates, stopped and said, "Cathy, Marianne, hadn't you better start if you're going to catch the ferry? It leaves in about ten minutes."

"You're going to the mainland?" Don asked Marianne.

She nodded. "To have a shake and maybe go to a movie."

"What's on?" Andy asked.

"Some kind of spy thing," Marianne said.

"R rating?" Don asked.

"If it's rated R," Granny said, "none of you goes. Is that clear?" She put down the plates. "I think I'll just investigate." She went past us out into the hall and picked up the telephone book. "There's one thing to be said for having just one theater, it simplifies matters. Here it is." She dialed and we all stood there like lumps.

"Hello?" she said into the receiver. "Will you tell me what's playing this afternoon and what its rating is?" Pause. "Thank you." She put down the receiver. "Marianne was quite right. It's an old spy movie. I've seen it and it's perfectly all right for you to go."

Marianne smiled. "It should be a lot of fun." It had never occurred to me before, but I noticed now that she had a dimple in her right cheek. In fact, she was quite pretty.

120

"Let's go then," Don said.

"Yeah," Andy agreed. "That'd be terrific."

For a second I felt rotten, so rotten that I wanted to cry. The next minute I wanted to kill everybody, especially Marianne. I opened my mouth. "I—"

"Cathy, could you come here a minute? I want to give you an errand for me. Come along now, I'm in a hurry." Granny appeared in the doorway, put her hand on my shoulder, shoved me back into the dining room and closed the door. Then she opened it again and put her head out. "Cathy will be with you in a minute. Why don't you wait on the porch?"

"Now you come into the kitchen with me, Cathy. I want to talk to you." And before I knew what she was doing, she pushed open the swing door and pulled me into what used to be the pantry. "Cathy, I could tell by the look on your face that you were about to explode. Don't do it. Go along with them. Go to the movies. Pretend nothing's wrong."

"Andy's a fink! He won't even invite me to play with him and Don!"

"Right now he's going to do whatever Don wants to do. And Don is plainly taken with Marianne."

"Well, why won't Don let me be with them? It's him that doesn't want me."

"Because you live here. If he encouraged you to play with them once, they'd be stuck with you—he thinks— for the rest of his stay here. Marianne comes from the outside, so it's a bit different. And, as I said, he's taken with her. Darling, don't cry! It's not worth it. I think perhaps Don also made up to Marianne because she's no threat to his influence over Andy. And maybe he thinks you are. These things are not simple. If you show how hurt you are, it will just give all three satisfaction. It's a dreary thing to say about human nature, but it's true."

"Isn't pretending just like lying?" I said. "You said lies were wrong. They . . . they made things different."

Granny sighed. "Yes, I did. Here." She pulled a piece of paper toweling off the roller and handed it to me. I wiped my cheeks and blew my nose. "I shouldn't tell you what to do," Granny said. "You must do what you want and feels right. But I want you to take a couple of minutes out and think what you really want to do—for your own sake, for your own best good."

"I thought the ferry was going to leave any second," I said.

"That was just an excuse to try and head off what I could see coming."

"You mean you thought Don would invite Marianne?"

"I saw his face as he came downstairs. I also saw Marianne smile at him."

"She's a fink, too!"

"Darling, you might as well get used to it. When interest in the opposite sex comes into your life, almost everybody is capable of being what you call a fink. You, too."

"I don't think pretending is so different from lying." I looked up at Granny. "Is there any time ever you don't tell the *complete* truth?"

"Yes. When people who have no business doing so ask me my age."

"How old are you?"

Granny and I looked at each other, eyeball to eyeball. "I am fifty-nine."

I blew my nose again. "That's pretty old. Still, I

thought grandmothers were at least seventy and wore glasses."

"I wear contacts. And I'm not seventy. But I am definitely a grandmother. And you're my only grandchild, so I am just as besotted about you as most grandparents are about their children. Now go out and *act*. . . . If you pretend you don't care, or are even enjoying yourself, you'll take away whatever power the others have over you. And you might even start to enjoy yourself."

She leaned over and hugged me and kissed the top of my head.

"The trouble is, I'm not Number One with anybody," I said. "Daddy likes Laura better than me, and Laura has Andy, and Andy has Ruggles and Don, and Laura—"

"You are Number One—*Numero Uno*—with me. That is official."

"What about Daddy? He's your son."

"I still like you best."

I felt much better and decided I'd go out and be so nice they'd all eat worms. "Thanks," I said, and hugged Granny back. "I won't tell anyone your age, and fifty-nine really isn't that old."

"You are too kind," Granny murmured. But she was smiling.

Pretending didn't turn out to be as hard as I remembered, maybe because I really did start having a good time. Don was the one who suggested racing along the beach, and I beat them all, even Andy. We had shakes at the drugstore and then went to the movie, which turned out to be pretty good. After the movie we went back to the drugstore for more ice cream, and stayed there for a while, talking, so it was fairly late by the time Marianne said she had to go home for dinner.

We came out into the small common, which is really just a long triangle of grass. It was late in the afternoon and the sun was slanted way down, shining on the common between the houses and the trees. Next to the drugstore is the parish hall of one of the village's three churches. The lights were on in there, and a door at the side was open.

We were about to head towards the ferry when a tall figure that had been walking towards us on the common crossed the street and came up to where we were standing. The sun was in my eyes, so I couldn't see who it was until she was right next to us.

"Hello, Cathy."

I was so stunned, I could hardly open my mouth to say anything. For some reason, I never thought about Elizabeth being anywhere else but her house on the island. And how could I keep it a secret from Marianne if she walked up to me like that?

"Hi," I said. And then, "Come on, Marianne. It's late. Your mother'll be furious if you don't get home soon."

Elizabeth stood for a minute, as though I had hit her. Then she turned and went up the steps of the parish hall.

"That was the Wicked Witch," Marianne said. "You never told me you knew her."

"No, it isn't," I said. "Come on."

"It is too. Mother saw her once across the common when I was with her and pointed her out. You couldn't miss how tall she is."

124

"Who's the Wicked Witch?" Don asked.

"She's a crazy woman who collects animals and paints and lives by herself on the island. Mother won't let me go anywhere near her."

"Why not?" Don asked.

"Mother hasn't told me. But she knows something terrible about her."

"We're going to miss the ferry," I said. I was feeling awful because I wasn't sticking up for Elizabeth.

"There's one every twenty minutes at this time," Andy said. "You've been on the island more than I have. How come you don't know that?"

"Who wants to know how often the ferry goes? It's boring!"

"I wonder why she's going into the church?" Marianne said. "Mother and I belong to that church and we've never seen her before."

"Maybe she's going to be de-witched," Don said.

Marianne giggled.

"Let's go and see what's happening there," Don said.

"Yeah, let's," Andy said.

"Come on, Andy," I yelled. "Why do you have to do everything Don says?"

Don ran lightly up the steps of the hall. Andy went right behind him, and Marianne was behind Andy. There didn't seem to be anything else to do, so I went there, too.

"Wow, man!" Don said, looking at a sign hung just inside the door. "An AA meeting."

"You mean that car club?" Marianne said.

"No, silly. It's for drunks." He staggered around the steps and hiccoughed a couple of times. Then he grinned. "You know, 'My name is Joe Schmo and I am an alcoholic.' 'Hi, Joe,' they all yell back. Like in the movie,

The Days of Wine and Roses. Let's all go in and listen. We have an AA meeting at home. My uncle belongs. Sometimes some of us kids used to hide in the balcony and listen to them. It's a gas."

"I don't want to go. I don't think we ought to," I said.

"So go home, if that's the way you feel."

I could feel my knees shaking. "Marianne, you know your mother wouldn't want you to be here."

"Why not?" Don said. He turned to Marianne. "Did she ever tell you *not* to go to an AA meeting?"

Marianne shook her head. "No, never."

"But she wouldn't want you to go," I said. "You know how strict she is."

"Well . . ." Marianne looked doubtful.

"Come on, Marianne," Don said, and smiled at her. "You just said she didn't say you shouldn't. You don't want to be chicken, like Cathy here."

"I'm *not* chicken," I said, feeling desperate. "I just don't think we ought to go."

"I don't see why Mother wouldn't want me to be here," Marianne said. "Especially as she never told me I couldn't." She glanced at Don, then back at me, and suddenly sounded much bolder. "I think it'd be fun. Besides, you know the Wicked Witch and you never told me and I think you're mean!"

"You know her?" Don said.

"No," I lied.

"Well, she knows you. She walked right up and said 'Cathy.' "

I shrugged as coolly as I could, although my legs were shaking more than ever and I felt a little sick. "I've met her."

"She didn't say hello like somebody you'd just met," Don said. "Did she, Marianne?"

I looked at Andy for help. He muttered, "You meet lots of people up here. Why don't we go back? I'm hungry."

"After two shakes and a sundae?"

"Well, Grandma told us to be back for dinner."

"Look, do you always do what Grandma says?" Don spoke with a slight sneer.

It was funny, I thought. That was exactly what I always said to Marianne.

"Well," Don said. "Marianne and I are going in, aren't we?" He looked at Andy. "Come on!"

I looked at Andy, too. "Let's go home," I said.

He just stood there for a minute. Then he muttered, "We'll just go for a minute. Grandma'll keep dinner."

"She's not your grandma, she's mine," I said. "And I think we ought to be home for dinner."

"You're getting awfully full of law and order all of a sudden," Andy said. "At home you're always the one doing something that you've been told not to do. Well, right now I want to go to this AA meeting. If you want to go home, go." And he stepped into the small lobby outside the parish hall itself.

I stood there in the doorway, watching them. Don peered into the room, then looked back. "They're some stairs right ahead. Let's wait and see if they turn off some lights."

Just as he spoke, the lights in front of us went out.

"Come on," Don whispered.

We were all wearing sneakers. I followed them to the doorway to the main hall and saw the staircase opposite. Don, Marianne and Andy went up together. I stood there at the back of the hall. The shades were slanted, so it was dim except for the front where the lights were on. The grown-ups were much farther in front, sitting on chairs. There were a lot of them. Some man was going to a lectern.

"Good evening," he said. "My name is David and I am an alcoholic."

I waited for them all to yell back the way Don said, but they didn't.

I took a step forward, trying to see Elizabeth. There she was, right in the front row. I could see her tall fair head rising above most of the others. Then somebody in the back row started to turn around. I flew across the back of the room and up the stairs. The others were in the shadows upstairs all crouched down, just their eyes above the backs of some chairs. I didn't go down with them, but stayed behind a chair in back of them. I felt strange. My feelings were jumbled up. I was excited, curious and afraid.

"And now," the man downstairs said, "I'll introduce our first speaker, Elizabeth."

As Elizabeth got up, I saw she had on a blue dress, and the one ceiling light left on shone down on her honey-colored, straw-colored hair. There was a standing lamp beside her, so that the short, curly strands of hair looked as though they stood out.

"Good evening," she said. "My name is Elizabeth and I am an alcoholic."

Alcoholic meant drunk, I thought, as her voice switched on and off in my head. And drunk meant. . . . Suddenly, in my memory, I again smelled Gunn's breath. Although I couldn't remember exactly why, I knew I didn't like it. In fact I hated it, and for the same reason

—whatever it was—I hated peppermint. The two smells seemed to go together, and they went with loud voices that screamed. The smells, the sounds, sprang into my head as though I had invented them. But I knew I hadn't. At that moment I was certain that at some time they had been part of my life. I couldn't actually remember it, but, as though a door were slowly opening, I knew . . .

I tried to concentrate on what Elizabeth was saying, but my heart was beating like a hammer and I had stomach cramps. I took a deep breath. The others were giggling quietly. By this time I could see better in the dark, and I saw Marianne turn around and look at me . . .

". . . in the last and worst of my drinking," Elizabeth was saying, "when my daughter was about four, I would scream at her, abuse her verbally. . . . A lot of it I don't remember . . . I was told about it. What I do remember is her fear, her revulsion, when I first came to see her after I got sober. That was the last time I saw her until . . . Her father was given complete custody, and has forbidden any contact. . . ."

Somehow I got down the stairs and managed to wait until I reached the sidewalk before I started being sick. But when people came over to see what the matter was, I ran. I ran and I ran and I ran. That nightmare I'd always had was back there in the hall. . . . A creature in a blue robe, with straw-colored hair, coming after me.

eight

Afterwards, somebody—I think it was Granny—asked me what I was thinking as I ran to the pier and onto the ferry, and then off the ferry onto the island and across the beach road up to the hill and up to the cliff. And the truth is, I can't remember thinking anything. I just ran. When I got to the cliff point with the shelf beneath it, I climbed down onto the shelf and sat with my back to the little half-cave right under the overhanging cliff, where no one from above could see me as long as I kept my feet under me. And then I felt safe.

I don't know how long I sat there. I just stared at the sea, which grew steadily more purple as the sun, which was behind me and behind the cliff, started to go down. I thought about the sun and the sea and the fishing boats and the direction I was facing, because I did not want to think about Elizabeth or the AA meeting or the woman in my nightmare or Granny or anything.

"The sun rises in the east and sets in the west," I said to myself, aloud. I knew the island ran sort of northeast to southwest. The cliff shelf faced the ocean. There was more sun on my right side than on my left. And on my left the water was a much deeper purple than on my right. So I was probably facing southeast. I looked at my watch and discovered that it had stopped at one-thirty because I'd forgotten to wind it. Well, I thought, it would be easy to calculate the time by working backwards. We'd been to a movie and had shakes before and ice cream afterwards, and then gone to the parish—but I wrenched my mind away from that because the shaking inside me started the moment I let myself think about seeing and hearing Elizabeth in that parish room. . . . The movie must have lasted an hour and a half, because movies usually did, unless they were long ones. Then there were the ferry trips—say another thirty minutes—and the walk to the ferry and my run . . . and what time did we start? I'd come back from Elizabeth's—but with even the thought of her name my mind slid immediately to Elizabeth in the parish hall, speaking words I didn't want to think about, the light behind her making her hair look like a straw halo . . . I started to shake again and yanked my mind away and back to calculating what time it was. Taking everything together, it might be around five-thirty. Which meant it wouldn't get dark for another two hours. And in those two hours people would come looking for me. But who knew I would be here? Andy, unless he was so busy being chums with Don he wouldn't think or care. Granny, because she knew about the first time I hid here. And Elizabeth?

This time I couldn't get my mind off the dangerous topic. It was true that Elizabeth didn't know I'd once hidden on this shelf. But she lived a short way away, down the side of the cliff and up the other side. Would she know about the shelf? Would she have looked over and discovered it?

Elizabeth, I told myself—the Elizabeth whom I had known in her cottage and with whom I had painted—that Elizabeth was not the woman in the nightmare. It was just an accident that I had looked at her under the light and listened to her and panicked.

"She's not the same person," I said aloud, and discovered that my teeth were chattering. Was I cold? I tried to feel my arms under my sweat shirt and sweater. I was shaking, but I really didn't know whether I was cold or not. Elizabeth was my friend. She'd taught me to paint and draw. She was going to give me one hundred and forty-five dollars at the end of the month, which would more than pay for my bicycle. Why did I think she was the woman in the blue robe? If she was not the woman in the blue robe, why did I feel so terrified and sick when I thought about her?

All of a sudden and for the first time, I looked down. Far below were the rocks. The tide was going out and the sea, with white foam, was lashing itself against the rocks below. Why on earth was I here? I could die, especially if I waited until dark to try and climb up. But surely somebody would have thought to look under the cliff by the . . . Or would they? . . . Did I want to be found?

Yes. No.

Not thinking about something is very hard, I discovered. I couldn't bear to think about Elizabeth, because I then thought immediately about the woman in the blue robe in my dream. And when I did that, I started to shiver again. Yet even as much as I didn't want to think about her, my mind kept going back to her. I would think about Elizabeth standing there in the parish hall, with the blue dress on and the light making her yellowish hair stick out, talking about her daughter. Then I would know that the other woman was somewhere in the back of my head, and unless I was very careful, she would be right there, in front where I could see her.

"Why?"

I pushed the thought of her away again and made

myself think instead about Granny and Marianne and Andy and Daddy and Laura and school back in New York and Janet crewing for her brother in Long Island. I even thought hard about Mrs. Proudy with her flutey voice and phony way of saying things. But somehow that brought me back to Marianne's saying to Andy and Don that her mother wouldn't let her have anything to do with the Wicked Witch . . . and there the Wicked Witch was, coming over the common, right up to where we were standing, and saying "Hello, Cathy" in a voice that I had known somewhere, somehow, a long time ago.

I opened my eyes, which had been closed, because I was sure the sun must have gone down, I was so cold. But the sun was as bright as ever. . . . Maybe it was because I was sitting high up on a cliff on the windward side of the island. Granny was always telling me to take a sweater because it would be cold. . . .

I would be much happier running, I decided. It was easy to run. I was good at it. And when you ran you didn't have to think. . . . But if I got up and climbed to the top of the cliff so I could run somewhere, everybody would find me, because right now they were all coming after me like the woman in the dream. . . . And anyway, if I got up and climbed to the top, then I would never find out if they would bother to look for me. . . . A terrible sense of confusion filled me.

I switched my thoughts to MacDuff with his big tan head and gentle manner. I could do a book about Mac-Duff. All by himself he'd be the hero. Elizabeth said my animals were good. . . . Elizabeth.

"No, no, no, no," I yelled, beating on the rock shelf with my hands.

"Who's up there?"

The voice came from below and to my right. I tried to uncross my legs so I could crawl on my tummy and look over. But I discovered my legs had gone to sleep and were full of pins and needles.

"Speak up, now, so I can hear yer. Who's there?"

Slowly, so I wouldn't wobble and fall over, I got my legs straightened. Then I turned onto my stomach and wiggled forward. At first I found myself looking straight into a tree that curved up out of the cliff side. Then I pushed myself to the left and saw them. There, in their boat, in the little cove underneath the point of the cliff, were Gunn and MacDuff.

"What are yer doin' up there? Yer must be daft!"

I was so glad to see them, I felt like shouting for joy. "Hello, Mr. Gunn! Hello, MacDuff!"

When I said his name, MacDuff barked. Then he stood up on the seat in the middle of the boat and barked again, and looked down at the water and whined.

"Be quiet! Sit!" Gunn roared.

MacDuff obeyed him, but kept whining and barking.

"How in the name of everything marvelous did yer get up there?"

"I didn't get up," I said, "I came down. There're lots of footholds. It's easy."

It was odd, I thought. I'd always heard that sound carried over water. This was the first time I'd found it to be true. I was far up the cliff and Gunn was down in his boat on the water, yet I really didn't have to yell. It was also funny how much better I felt knowing that Gunn knew I was there.

"Then go back up again. It's no place for yer to be. And it'll be dark soon. But wait. . . . There's rope in the boat down here. MacDuff and I'll go back to the pier then

134

walk up the other side and help yer. Don't move. Wait. We'll be there."

I saw him lean forward and take a long pull on one oar, bringing the boat around and heading it towards the pier on the other side of the cove.

I felt so much better, not shaking and not afraid. Getting up the cliff suddenly seemed very simple. "I can manage," I yelled. "There are lots of holds for the hands."

"Yer should wait now," Gunn yelled. But he stopped rowing for a minute and rested the oars, watching me.

I sat up, and then I stood up and turned and faced the cliff. Reaching up, I grasped a jutting stone and put my foot in a hole about ten inches above the shelf floor. I felt fine. Then, a second before it gave way, I knew the rock under my hand wouldn't hold and I tried to get my foot out so I could jump down to the shelf. But the lace of my sneaker got caught between two stones and my foot stuck for a few seconds. I fell backwards. I'm going to die, I thought, and because everything seemed to happen in slow motion, I seemed to have a lot of time to think about it as I fell to the shelf and slid off. The strange part was, I wasn't especially scared, not anywhere near as much as in my nightmare. I didn't even scream. But I heard Gunn shout and MacDuff bark and felt a terriffic blow and scraping all over my face and hands.

"Are you all right? Speak up, lassie, for God's sake!"

I was in the tree, cradled where the branches met. I was so sore I didn't think I'd ever want to move again. There was a branch straight above my head. Slowly, keeping my balance, I took hold of it with one hand, and then with another.

"Are you all right?" yelled Gunn.

"I'm okay," I yelled back. "I'm in the tree."

"You're not to move. You understand? I'll get help and ropes."

I was lying a little on one side, so I could turn my head and stare down. The rocks seemed much nearer, but it was still a long way down. "Maybe I could climb down," I said doubtfully.

"T'would be better if a rope could be lowered from the top."

I was about to agree when there was a crack just under me. I felt the trunk under my back move. "This is going to break," I yelled. "It just cracked."

"There's no way I can tie up the boat here," Gunn said. "And the tide's going out. If the boat drifts away, we'll be stuck on the rocks, and when the tide turns, the water covers them this side."

I pulled myself up a little by the branch over me. There was another crack. I stared down. How many feet was it to the bottom?

"Well, needs must," Gunn said. I could see him maneuver the boat close. Then he stood up and reached out for the rock. With both hands on it, he pulled the boat closer. Then he bent down and lifted the coil of rope at the bottom of the boat.

"Now just breathe easy. I'll get the rope around something and come after you."

I couldn't see too well what he was doing, and I didn't dare move.

I heard him scuffling below and moved my head a fraction. The coil of rope was lying on the rock. Gunn, now standing on the shore, was bending to reach the rope at the bow of the boat, the one he used to tie it to the pier. I realized what he meant then when he said there was no way to tie it. My neck was getting a crick in it, so I turned it back and looked straight out to sea. There were other boats, farther out: two fishing boats and what looked like a Coast Guard cutter. They were like dots, much too far away to see us. Then, when the crick eased, I turned back. Gunn was trying to push the boat's rope between two rocks to hold it. He gave it a final shove, then began to unwind the coil at his feet.

MacDuff started to jump onto the rock.

"Stay!" Gunn roared. "You'll just be in the way! Now," he yelled up at me, "I'll toss the rope up. Put it around the base of the tree where it joins the rock. Do you think you can do that?"

I eased up a little, waiting for another crack. But there wasn't one, and I was sitting up. "Yes, I think so. But what good will it do?"

"If the rope is looped over the tree and I'm holding it taut at the bottom, you can clamber down the rope. You can do that, can't you? You do it in the gym at home."

"Sure."

In a minute there was a flurry of leaves around me, and I made a snatch at where I thought the rope was, nearly losing my balance. Quickly I clutched at the branch above me.

"Now try and catch it," Gunn said. And I heard the flurry of leaves again. Again I missed it.

"I'm afraid of falling if I move too much," I said.

"I'll try and throw it a bit nearer."

This time the rope came straight up beside me. I grasped it and pulled up on it, bending the end down over the stump of the tree where it came out of the rock.

"Now send it—" Gunn started, when there was a frantic barking and whining. I turned quickly and heard the cracking of rotten wood.

"MacDuff!"

The rope had come loose and the boat was moving rapidly away from the rocks.

Gunn gave an anguished cry. "Jump! Jump, lad!"

But the tide was moving too quickly and the boat was drawing out of the cove. I suddenly remembered what Granny had said about the dangerous pull around the rocks. MacDuff, who was old, couldn't possibly swim against it.

"Stay! Stay!" Gunn roared this time. "Stay in the boat!"

But it was too late. The dog had looked at the water, whimpered once, and, obeying Gunn as he had all his life, jumped in.

"MacDuff!"

MacDuff swam hard, but the tide swirling around the point was stronger. I saw his head moving faster and faster out to sea, the boat drifting along with him. A frantic yelp came from him. I turned, and the tree broke. I screamed this time as I fell.

"Catch the rope!" Gunn yelled at me.

He must have pulled it tight as he cried out because, when I caught it, it was taut. And there I was, halfway between the stump of the tree, which was holding the hope, and Gunn, far beneath. He was holding the rope with both hands, but he was staring out to sea. MacDuff's head was barely visible now. Suddenly, faintly, over the water, came a yelp.

Evidently Gunn, watching MacDuff, had loosed his hold, because the rope started to give. I felt myself falling, and screamed again. "Don't let me fall! Don't let me fall!"

He tightened the rope. Slowly, inch by inch, I slid down the rest of the way, skinning my knuckles on the rock, terrified that Gunn would drop the rope and plunge after MacDuff. "Don't leave me!" I yelled twice.

Finally I got to where he could reach me, and he lifted me down to the rock. Then he stood staring out at the water. The boat was way out. MacDuff was not visible.

"MacDuff . . ." I said.

"He's gone." I saw the tears wet on Gunn's cheeks. "Ma old friend, I couldna help him."

A silent Gunn helped me off the rocks down to the beach and into his pickup. Then he drove me home. When I climbed out, I said to him, "I'm sorry. . . I'm truly sorry about MacDuff."

"Aye," he said, and drove off immediately.

It was dark now. Granny opened the door before I even started up the short path. Then she came quickly across the lighted porch and waited for me to come up the steps.

I stared up at her. She looked very angry or very worried or both.

"Cathy, where have you been?"

I opened my mouth and tried to say something. But a great pain was in my throat. Then I started to cry.

Granny came down the steps and put her arms around me.

"It's all right, Cathy. I know what happened. I got the story out of the boys and that silly Marianne. And then I talked to Elizabeth. I was going to tell you. Come in. You're cold."

"Oh, Granny," I said. "It's awful!"

"Yes, I know. I'll explain."

"MacDuff's dead. And it's my fault. He jumped into

the water, but the tide was going out and he couldn't swim against it. And Gunn just had to stand there because he was holding the rope and I was scared and so he couldn't help him. Oh, Granny! I wish I was dead!"

Granny didn't say anything for a minute. Then she said, "I see. It's MacDuff you're upset about. I thought— but it doesn't matter. She stroked my back and went on, "Come inside, Cathy. It's dark and it's getting chilly. You're shivering. I have some hot soup I want you to drink. Then you're going to take a hot bath. If you feel like it, we can talk afterwards."

I drank a few swallows of soup and then pushed it away.

"Granny," I said.

"First your bath. Come along, I'll run it for you."

"Where are the others?"

"I sent Andy and Don up to their bedroom to think over their behvaior. I don't like the way Andy's been treating you. And I don't like that Don at all. I made him telephone a relative tonight, and he's leaving tomorrow. But most of all, he had no right to induce you into that parish hall. Those people have a right to their privacy. And I gave Marianne a piece of my mind, too."

All this time we were walking upstairs. Granny went into the bathroom next to my room and turned on the taps. "Now," she said. "Take your clothes off and get in."

I didn't realize how cold I was until I slid into the hot water. Half an hour later, we were sitting in front of the fireplace in the living room.

Granny said, "I think it's cool enough for me not to feel guilty about lighting the fire. So let's light it."

While she was setting a match to the curls of newspaper, I sat on the floor with the quilt from my bed up-stairs around me, staring into the fire.

Granny sat down in the chair I was leaning against. "Tell me about MacDuff."

So I told her about him and about Gunn, and how MacDuff used to put his head on my lap and sometimes lick my ear and that his eyes were almost gold. "I liked him better than any other animal, Granny, and he liked me. I know he did. Gunn said so. He liked me better than anybody except Gunn, and he was much more affectionate to me than he was even to Gunn when we were all to-gether. And oh, Granny! He must have known that no-body was coming after him there in the sea and that Gunn, who he liked best of all, rescued me instead."

Granny touched my hair with her fingers. "Cathy darling, MacDuff sounds like a wonderful dog. But he *was* a dog, not a person—no, I don't mean that. He was a person, but not a human person. And animals don't think the same way humans do. So I don't think he thought Gunn was choosing you over him."

After a while I found a handkerchief in my robe pocket and blew my nose. But I couldn't stop crying.

"You know," Granny went on, "I'm sorrier than I can say that this happened. But I'm happy that you came to love an animal and to see how wonderful they can be. You've never cared for animals before. Ruggles is a nice dog, but you don't much like him, do you?"

I shook my head.

"Why? Do you know why, Cathy?"

I didn't say anything for a while. Then I said. "I guess it's because Andy always said he liked Ruggles better than me. Even before that though, I didn't much like animals."

141

"This is your old problem, isn't it? Not being Number One."

"I suppose so."

"Well, you're right. It didn't start with Ruggles. Which sort of brings me to Elizabeth. Do you . . . did you . . . recognize her?"

"She's like the woman in my dream, the one who chases me."

It was funny and sad, I thought. I felt so awful about MacDuff, I now couldn't feel as frightened of the woman in my dream as I had. Yet it was because of her that I ran to the cliff.

"Do you dream about her often?"

"Yes. Not all the time. But often."

"And when you saw Elizabeth tonight, did she remind you of the woman in your dream?"

"Yes. She had a blue dress and yellow hair . . . but the she-monster in my dream is ugly and huge and has a red face. . . ."

There was a fairly long silence. "Cathy," Granny said, "did you make any connection in your head between the woman in your dream and Elizabeth?"

There was that awful confusion again. I closed my eyes.

But I knew what she was talking about. I had known it since this afternoon and maybe since before that. "She's the woman I dream about, the she-monster, isn't she?"

"Did you find her a monster when you went up to her studio on top of the hill?"

"No, but she's the same, isn't she?"

"Did Elizabeth say anything about her daughter this afternoon?"

"Yes. She said when her daughter was four she

screamed at her . . ." I didn't even think about the next question before it popped out of my mouth. "Granny, when did my mother die?"

"She didn't die, Cathy. I know you were told that, or allowed to think it, but it isn't true. She got sick. I told you that once, remember? Alcoholism is a disease. It's a disease like any other disease. When she became her sickest, your father took you away and later got a divorce."

"But why did everybody say she was dead?" I forgot about holding the quilt around me and started to stand up. "Granny, Elizabeth's my mother, isn't she? I'm the kid she was yelling at. Why didn't you tell me? I don't think it's fair. I think it was sneaky and mean not to let me know."

"Sit down, Cathy. I want you to keep warm." When I had sat down again and pulled the quilt around me, she said, "Nobody meant to be unfair to you or sneaky. Your father just thought it was easier and less complicated for you to let you believe this lie—at least until you were older. I think he was wrong, though I understand his bitterness. But now you can see why I believe that lies, in the long run, cause more trouble than they help."

"It was Daddy, wasn't it, who told me she was dead?"
"Yes."

"Well, I don't see why you haven't told him about lies and how you feel about them."

"Listen, Cathy, remember another thing I said to you? About not judging? Sometimes, when what people do hurts us, it's not easy not to judge. But you have to keep on trying. Alcoholism is not a pretty disease. It makes people do things they'd never do otherwise. Like your mother shouting at you." Granny paused. "I think one reason you've always had this distrust of animals is that she had a poodle, and when she'd been drinking, she had a habit of asking you if you loved her. I know because I walked in on a scene like that once. And, of course, she wanted reassurance from you when you felt least like giving it. So when you rebuffed her, or she thought you did, she'd fuss over her poodle to make you jealous. 'Patti loves me more than you do . . .' she'd say. And she'd hug and kiss Patti while you stood there and glared at them both. Then, of course, she'd get angry and start screaming at you. She did the same to your father. And, while he knew it was her disease that made her behave like that, he became bitter and angry.

"About a year after you went to live with your father, she went into a rehabilitation place and finally managed to stop drinking. She came to see you then, twice. But each time you ran screaming out of the room. Do you remember that, Cathy? You were about six."

Something stirred, something unpleasant. There was a room and a woman and the noise of myself screaming and running. But it was like my dream. I shook my head. "Not really."

"Well, it was after that that your father managed to get the court to refuse her any right to see you and encouraged you to believe that she had died. As I said, I think he was very wrong. Apart from anything else, he knew that sooner or later you'd find out the truth. But when I pointed that out to him, he said that when you were older it wouldn't matter. Anyway, he has stubbornly stuck to his deception. . . . Cathy, I don't mean to criticize him to you or give you grounds for being upset with him. He's my son, he's a fine man and I love him. But he has been bitterly hurt and he had several years of horror as Elizabeth's drinking increased, and with it her injury to you. There's justice on both sides. . . . As for Elizabeth—she was shattered not only by her own guilt, but by your reception of her. It told her more about her behavior towards you when she was drinking than she would have accepted from anyone else. After that she went out to the West Coast to try and put her life together. She started painting out there, met George O'Byrnne, married him and went abroad with him for several years.

"I thought she'd put aside her desire to see you, accepted the fact that she couldn't. Then she took the old seaman's house on the hill as her studio, and when she knew you were going to come up here, asked me to let her see you. I told her I wouldn't set it up—wouldn't arrange it, so to speak. But if you happened to meet her one way or another, then I wouldn't stop it. . . . I didn't feel quite honest about it. But then I didn't feel quite right about refusing. So I let it go at that and was wondering how she could contrive the meeting. Who would have thought Marianne would have been the *deus ex machina*."

"The *what?*"

"Literally, the god in the machine. It comes from the days of Greek drama. The god—an actor—was lowered onto the stage in a sort of box and he would then untwist the plot, or resolve the problem, or offer a way out of a situation. Now it just means some outside agency coming in to do the same."

I giggled for a minute at the idea of Marianne being lowered in a box. But then I asked, "But why didn't she tell me she was my mother? It's the kind of thing a person would like to know."

"Because she didn't know how much you remembered, how much you could still feel fear and hatred of her. The way she put it was that she wanted to meet you, just as two people, without the emotional load your knowing about the relationship would carry. And that was what was happening. You were coming to like her, weren't you?"

"Yes." I thought a little. "Sort of. She was helping me with my book."

"I knew about your drawings, but I didn't know about your book. Tell me about it."

So I told her about my story about the island and Gunn and his boat and MacDuff, Head Dog, and Ruggles, Slave Dog, and Andy in the dungeon proposing to me every day and me refusing him. "And now MacDuff's dead and Gunn's boat is gone and he won't be able to fish, and that horrible woman in my dream turns out to be my mother. I think Daddy was right. I wish I'd never known her. It's all her fault."

Granny put her hand on my head again. "No, it's not all her fault. I know how you feel, but it's not all her fault. We all had a share in it."

We sat there in the silence for a while. There was a lovely smell from the wood burning. After a while, the fire collapsed inward and went down to a red glow.

"I'll put one more piece on," Granny said. She got up and took a log from the log holder and put it on the fire. Then she came back and sat down in the chair again.

After another long silence, she said, "Elizabeth would like to see you again tomorrow morning. Do you think you could go up there to see her?"

"No. I don't want to."

"Well, I won't insist. I can't. I just wish . . . I wish

things had turned out better. For you both. But especially for her."

"You sound like you like her."

"I do. I've always liked her. I didn't like what she became when she drank, and I was extremely angry at her for what she did to you and your father. But she's always been interesting and bright and full of courage. And I admire how she's turned herself around. She's very much a person."

"I won't go."

"All right. But I *am* going to insist that you now go to bed. You should be worn out."

We got up. Granny put the mesh screen around the fire, then she folded the quilt and said, "Up! I'll follow you."

After I'd put the quilt back on my bed and brushed my teeth, I said, "Granny, can I sleep with you tonight?"

"All right. Go along and get into my bed."

I went to sleep almost right away. This time I dreamed about MacDuff. He was sitting in Gunn's boat in the middle of the ocean, looking alive and well and waiting for us to come and get him. I was so glad to see him, I started to call out to him. The only funny thing was, in my dream he wasn't a he. MacDuff was a she. Anyway, I dreamed I was calling his-her name. Then I woke up. It was dark and Granny was on the other side of the big bed.

"What's the matter, darling?" Granny asked.

"I dreamed about MacDuff. I don't want him to be dead."

"I know you don't."

I lay there for a while. Then I said, "Granny, would you please sing 'Passengers Will Please Refrain'?"

Granny sang it through twice for me. We both giggled a little and then I went to sleep.

"Are you sure you don't want to go to Elizabeth's studio this morning?" Granny said at breakfast.

"I'm positive."

"What about that money you were so keen for?"

I had been thinking about the money and the bicycle. Granny, I noticed, was looking closely at me. Finally I said, "Well, I'll just have to not have it."

When I thought about MacDuff, the bicycle didn't seem that important. I pushed the rest of my cereal away. "I'm going to go down to the beach."

"To see Gunn?"

"Yes."

"If he doesn't have his boat, will he be there?"

"I don't know. But I'm going anyway."

"All right."

Just as I was about to go out the front door, Granny came out of the living room and said, "Do you mind if I go with you? I haven't seen Gunn in a long time and I'd like to thank him for rescuing you. I'd call him, but I know he doesn't have a phone in that hovel of his."

"What's a hovel?"

"A dilapidated shack."

I really wanted to go alone. But then I thought that Granny didn't have to ask. She could have just come along with me. "Okay," I said.

You can get to the beach from around the point behind our house, instead of over the hill and down the other side, which was the way I usually took since I always went to the beach from Elizabeth's studio. This time Granny and I went around the point and walked along the rocky shore until we finally came to the beach.

I don't know what I expected to see when we got to the beach: maybe Gunn sitting on the rocky pier at the other end, staring out to sea. I certainly didn't expect to see him about to launch his boat with MacDuff sitting there in it.

For a minute I just stood still, staring, wondering if I was in the middle of one of my dreams. Then, "MAC-DUFF!" I screamed and started running. "MacDuff, Mac-Duff!" I kept yelling. "I thought you were dead!"

MacDuff never ran to greet me before, but this time he jumped out of the boat and loped slowly towards me, his legs moving stiffly. I knelt down and hugged and kissed him and felt him lick my face. Then we rolled over in the sand together.

When we finally got up and MacDuff stood and shook the sand off himself, Gunn was walking slowly towards us, grinning.

"Aye," he said. "They found them both, together. The boat must have drifted nearer to MacDuff and he took hold of the rope and held on, the clever dog! The Coast Guard saw the boat and turned on the searchlight, and then saw MacDuff and pulled him and the boat aboard. They dried him off and brought him to me last night. I woulda called yer, but I didn't have the phone. How do yer do," he said, looking at Granny. Then he took off his cap. It was a shock to see he was bald.

"Hello, Mr. Gunn. I came to thank you for rescuing my granddaughter. It was wonderful of you. Especially since MacDuff was in trouble, too, and I know how you feel about him. I'm so glad he's alive and all right."

"Ach, he's a grand dog! There's none like him. He was a wee bit tired when they brought him last night. But he's fine now." Gunn put his cap back on. "Would yer lak to go fer a row?"

"Thank you," Granny said. "I'm sure Cathy would. But I have an errand. Cathy, I'll see you back for lunch."

Somehow I knew Granny was going up to see Elizabeth. But I didn't say anything and neither did she.

When I got back to the house for lunch, Andy was there but Don had gone. I decided to ignore Andy and talked to Granny almost entirely about MacDuff and Gunn.

"I thought you didn't like dogs," Andy said finally.

"I don't. But I like MacDuff. He's a German shepherd."

"He's not pure bred," Andy said.

"He is too. Anyway, how would you know?"

"Because I've seen him. He's got something else in him."

"He does not!"

"It doesn't matter whether he does or not," Granny said. "Both of you, calm down. Cathy, MacDuff is a magnificent dog. It doesn't matter whether he's one breed or six. And Andy, why don't you stop making negative comments?" She stared at him for a minute. "Ruggles is a good dog, too."

The next morning I got a letter from Laura saying

she and Daddy had had a wonderful time but were looking forward to getting up to the island, and that they'd
arrive the following Monday, almost a week away. Granny
had a letter, too, from Daddy.

I went out rowing with Gunn and MacDuff every
morning for the rest of the week. In the afternoons
Granny, Andy and I would go swimming and would have
a picnic on the beach. The water was still very cold, but
we'd play games and often Ruggles and MacDuff would
play with us.

And all the time I knew Elizabeth was waiting for
me up in her house, hoping I would come to see her.
I kept expecting Granny to say something, to tell me I
should go, so I could refuse. But she didn't say anything
at all.

Then one afternoon Andy said, "Look, I'm sorry
about . . . well, about that afternoon at that meeting. I
didn't stick up for you, and I should have."

I shrugged and didn't say anything. It was nice to
have Andy wanting to be friends with me for a change,
instead of the other way around.

But Granny heard him say it and later, when he went
back for a second dip in the water, she said to me, "You
know, Andy did the handsome thing and apologized. I
think you could be generous enough to say it was okay."

I stared down at my feet and shook some sand onto
one foot with the other. "If Don came back, he'd like him
better," I said.

"Perhaps. But you can't stop being friends with
people just because you're not Number One with everybody all the time. I know he's Number One with you,
but—"

"He isn't any more."

"All right. But I still think you ought to consider forgiving him."

"I don't know what forgiving really means. Does it mean I pretend it never happened?"

"No. You just accept whatever it is and go on from there and don't build up a great resentment." After a minute, Granny went on, "After all, Gunn could have not forgiven you for getting in a jam on the cliff so that he had to choose between helping you or helping MacDuff."

"MacDuff didn't drown."

"But Gunn thought he did. So the spirit of it remains the same. And if you hadn't run away and climbed down the cliff and then fallen, MacDuff would never have been in danger. But you did, and he was, and Gunn rescued you, and when it looked like he'd lost an old friend because of it, he didn't reproach you, did he?"

I shook my head.

"Will you think about it?"

"All right."

So I thought about that off and on for the rest of the week. Finally Friday came. I knew Daddy and Laura would come on Monday. After that, things would be different.

I managed to leave the house Friday morning without anybody asking me where I was going. First I went around to the beach and talked to Gunn and MacDuff. But I didn't go rowing with them. I climbed up the hill and knocked on Elizabeth's door.

There was a terrific noise of barking inside. When Elizabeth opened the door, Jason hurled himself against me and Susan wound in and out of my legs. As I looked down at her and remembered the noise I had made, I thought, She's forgiven me. Maybe, being an animal person instead of a human person, she just didn't remember it.

"Hello," Elizabeth said.

I looked up. "Hi."

"Come in."

I followed her into the studio.

"Susan's forgiven me," I said. "Or maybe she doesn't remember."

Elizabeth picked up a brush and started to clean it. "I don't think animals forgive or do not forgive. I think it just means she's forgotten. But if you had hurt her enough, she would remember and run from you, so maybe it's the same thing."

A silence fell. I didn't know what to say. Finally I said, "Can I have my book?"

"Yes. Here it is. I typed the script for you."

Elizabeth handed me the package of my paintings and my typed story.

There was something I wanted to say, but I didn't know what it was. Now that I knew that Elizabeth was my mother, I was afraid she'd burst into tears and cry all over me and hug me and kiss me and all that kind of thing.

But Elizabeth just went on cleaning her brushes.

Finally I said, "I know you're my mother."

"Yes. I know you do." She put down the brushes and looked at me. "I'm glad you came today. Because you didn't know before, I couldn't tell you how sorry I am about all the wrong things I did, and all the right things I didn't do when we lived together. It's past now and there's nothing I can do about it. Maybe . . . maybe sometime in the future I can make up for it in some way."

"It's all right," I muttered, and thought suddenly about Andy.

"No, it isn't really." She paused. "I know your father doesn't want me to see you, and I can't blame him—much. I'm not criticizing him. But if he will change his mind, then perhaps we can be friends."

Susan had jumped up on the table and I stroked her. I was beginning to feel better. Elizabeth wasn't going to rush over to me and make a big fuss.

After a minute I said, "Do you live in New York?"

"Yes. We do now."

"Maybe you can teach me to draw."

She smiled then, and moved a little, so that the light fell on her cheeks and I could see she'd been crying. "I think that'd be fun."

"I'll ask Daddy."

"All right. By the way, I owe you money for sitting for me. I've written out a check. I was going to send it to your grandmother. Here it is."

She held it out and I took it. But instead of feeling marvelous about the bicycle, I felt funny. "Maybe I shouldn't take this," I said.

"Why not? It was a professional agreement."

"All right." I stared at the figures. "But I didn't come the full time."

"It doesn't matter."

"Thanks," I said. I still didn't feel right about the check, but I didn't know what to do about it. "I'd better go now. Are you going to be here the rest of the summer?"

"No. My husband is coming home. I'm going to meet him, and then we're going on a trip."

I blurted out, "Is he Number One with you?"

She looked at me and smiled a little. "I'm not going to answer that. But I will tell you that I love him very much and I love you very much. Is that something you think about a lot? Being Number One?"

I nodded.

"Well, I certainly recognize it. It was a preoccupation with me most of my life and got me into a lot of trouble."

"Don't you still want it?"

"I'm so glad to be alive and sane and sober and have work that I love and people I love who love me, that I don't think about it the way I used to. Occasionally, but not often."

I moved toward the door. "Thanks a lot for the book. And for the check." I paused. "I'll see you in New York."

"I'll look forward to that."

When I got back to the house for lunch, Andy was playing with Ruggles in the yard.

"Andy," I said.

He looked up. "Yeah?"

"It's okay. About that afternoon."

He grinned. "Yeah, well. Thanks."

That evening Andy went to have dinner and spend the night with a friend on the mainland. After dinner, when it was dark, Granny and I went out and sat on the flat rock under the house and looked at the lights and the stars and smelled the water. I told her about my visit to Elizabeth.

"That's good," she said. "I'm glad you went."

"Do you think Daddy will let me see her in New York?"

"I have a strong feeling that you and I and Laura together will be able to persuade him."

"I like Laura a lot."

"So do I. So much for the traditional wicked stepmother!" She paused, and then said, "Cathy, now that you know Elizabeth is your mother, do you remember her at all?"

"No—not Elizabeth. I remember there was *someone*, but I don't remember *her*. Sometimes I'd try and imagine what she was like, and I'd imagine this terrific person who was always on my side. Which is pretty funny, now that I know what she was really like."

"Well, there's no need to be disillusioned about Elizabeth as she is today. I told you—she has wonderful qualities. You'll get to know them as you come to know her."

"Isn't now too late for finding a mother? I mean, for it to be real?"

"Now is never too late for good things to happen."

We sat there for a while without saying anything. After a bit, one of the words Granny had used pushed itself to the front of my mind: disillusioned.

"That's it, Granny! That's the fourth dragon Laura talked about and said you'd overcome. Disillusionment. Don't you remember? The other three were death and fear and pain. And you said you'd had all three because of Grandfather and your daughter drowning. What were you disillusioned about?"

Granny didn't answer at first. Then she said, "Some things are easier to explain to grown-ups, Cathy. I guess the best way I can describe it is that for a while . . . once . . . I wasn't sure that with your grandfather I was still Number One."

"You mean he had a girl friend? In a late TV movie I saw one night, when Laura thought I was in bed, there was this husband—"

"I'm not going to discuss it any further, Cathy. Is that clear?" Granny spoke sharply.

"Okay," I said.

There was another silence. Then Granny said, "The important thing is that we had a wonderful marriage and loved each other a lot."

I thought for a while. "Does everybody have to meet the four dragons?"

"Yes, in one way or another, sooner or later. But then there are the four good dragons."

"What are they?"

"Joy and love and work and friends."

"I don't know why work is such a good dragon."

"Didn't you enjoy doing your book?"

"Yes."

"Well?"

That made me remember the check Elizabeth had given me. I told Granny about it and about the bicycle without rules that I was going to get.

"What rules?" Granny asked.

I realized I should have kept my mouth shut. If I had thought about it, I'd have known Granny'd be sure to agree with Daddy's rules.

"What rules?" Granny asked again.

So I told her.

I was right. Granny agreed with Daddy. "I don't think there's anything outrageous in not wanting you to ride in the street where some car can knock you down or on the sidewalks where you can knock other people down. And Cathy, if you think your father is not going to lay down the same laws regardless of who bought the bicycle, then you don't know him as well as you should."

"But if it's *my* bicycle, bought with *my* money, what can he do?"

"He can take it back to the store or lock it in a room just the way I would."

"You would?"

"You bet I would. Until I got your promise. If you won't agree to sensible regulations about your safety, then he has to see that you do. One of you has to be responsible."

"Other kids ride on the sidewalk."

"How well I know! I've been nearly knocked over twice." After a minute she said, "Is riding in the park so bad?"

"No, I guess not."

"It's just the principle of the thing?"

"Yes."

"Why don't you save all that fire and passion for when you're really right? I see lots of people in the park on bikes. Many of them exercise their dogs that way."

"Maybe I'll get a dog," I said. "One like MacDuff."

"I'll make a pact with you. If you will promise your father to keep his rules, I'll see about a puppy as an early Christmas present."

"Oh, Granny, that would be wonderful!"

"But you'll have to be responsible for the puppy— the walking, feeding, training and cleaning up after. Okay?"

"Okay. I will."

"Agreed then? No riding your bike in the streets or on sidewalks? Just the park?"

"Agreed. Could you get a puppy like MacDuff, do you think?"

"He's pretty special, but I dare say we can try for something near."

"Granny," I said, after another while. "Could I come and live with you?"

"You can come and stay whenever you like as long as you like. But you know your father loves you very much and would want you to live most of the time with him."

"Yes, I guess so. I like him, too. And Laura. You know, I never really knew you properly till now, but—" I took a deep breath, "you're Number One with me."

Granny put her arm around me and gave me a squeeze. "As I told you, it's entirely mutual. And you can stay with me all you want. There's a room that'll be just yours. Okay?"

We sat there in silence for another while. The air was cool and a little damp and the water smelled of salt and fish and magic.

"Let's sing 'Passengers Will Please Refrain,'" I said.

So we sang it all the way through twice, including a new verse that Granny taught me. Then we went back home.

about the author

Isabelle Holland was born in Basel, Switzerland, where her father, a Foreign Service officer, was Consul. When she was three years old the family moved to Guatemala City, Guatemala, and when she was seven they moved to England, near Liverpool. She came to the United States at the age of twenty, to finish college at Tulane University, New Orleans. Since graduating from college, Ms. Holland has worked in New York City, mainly in publishing. She is the author of several books, both for children and adults. Among her books for young readers are *The Man Without a Face, Of Love and Death and Other Journeys,* and *Alan and the Animal Kingdom.* This is her first book for Lothrop, Lee & Shepard Books.